Other books by John Ney

for young people
OX: THE STORY OF A KID AT THE TOP

for adults
THE EUROPEAN SURRENDER

PALM BEACH: THE PLACE, THE PEOPLE,
ITS PLEASURES AND PALACES

WHITEY MCALPINE

Ox
Goes
North

Harper & Row, Publishers
New York, Evanston, San Francisco, London

Ox
Goes
North

More Trouble for
The Kid at the Top

by John Ney

For Mia
When one door closes, another opens

Ox
Goes
North

1

THE FIRST STORY I told was about how I had to write a composition on cows, and I had never seen one so my dad took me all over the United States and Mexico to find one. We never did, but we ran into plenty of other things. In that story I put a lot about what it's like to be rich and live in Palm Beach, and how Mom and Dad party around, and how lousy I feel most of the time.

Some people said they didn't believe some of the things that happened to me, and the way rich people live, but they are people who have never been there.

Anyhow, after that things were pretty calm for quite a while. I got out of the fourth grade and past fifth, sixth, and seventh and made it into eighth, which nobody expected. I'm still a year behind, but I'm not losing ground any more. I've grown a lot in the last couple of years and now I'm about six-four. I guess I'll be six-eight like my grandfather was—the one who made the money. I still weigh too much—I won't even say how much—but I'm not nearly as sloppy as I used to be. Everyone still calls me Ox, of course. I suppose I'll be Ox all my life. Once you're a big fat kid you're always remembered that way. I suppose I could slim down until I looked like Steve Cutter or some lifeguard at the B & T and I'd still be called Ox.

Dad and Mom are about the same. Dad still sleeps on the lawn when he can't make it all the way to the house, and Charles and I carry him inside in the morning the way we always have. Charles is still our chauffeur and he's just as mean and sarcastic as ever. Mom is still more interested in parties than anything else.

There are a few little differences. Dad had a big scare with his liver last year, and took up health foods and gave me a lot of lectures about how you and your body are the same thing, and a man should think of his body the same way he thinks of himself. I couldn't make much out of it. This last year he's been easing off the health foods, but he's still careful. He talks about pollution and saving wild animals, too.

I don't feel much better than I did three years ago, but I'm more used to feeling lousy. I talked to Mrs. Hollins about that a while ago, and asked her if she thought it was an improvement.

"I'd say so, Franklin," she said. She's my old fourth-grade teacher and maybe the best friend I've ever had. I still go down to talk to her when I want to be pretty honest.

"Maybe it's not an improvement," I said. "Maybe I'm just more used to it, like those people who get started on a life of crime or something and hate it, and then start finding it normal."

"That's a thought," she said. "But if you don't get used to the way you feel, you're going to be very miserable."

"And if I do get used to it, I'll feel great?"

"I don't think you'll ever go that far."

My problem is that I don't think there's any future for a kid today. I've said it before—if I live in Palm Beach and have everything, how come I feel so lousy? I'm the kid who has everything, and if I feel that lousy, how do the kids at the bottom feel? You can't even think about them.

We talked some more and then she said, "Nothing is simple, Franklin. Not even feeling lousy."

"What do you mean?"

"If I knew what I meant, I couldn't put it in words."

That's Mrs. Hollins. She can say a thing that seems to mean nothing, that you can't pin down at all, but then you think about it for a long time. Much longer than you think about what people have said when they hand you something complete.

It was June and school was just out when we had that talk. Normally I stay in Palm Beach for the summer and I like it. The place is not so crowded and you can do what you want. I get up late, watch TV for a while and then go to one of the clubs and lie around for the rest of the morning. After the B & T closes for the summer I usually go up to the Coral Beach. No matter what club I go to, though, I always have the same lunch—a lot of lobster salad and a couple of club sandwiches. In the afternoon I fool around with some other kids and at night I eat at home and then go out for a while. I usually see a late show on TV and get to bed about two.

People say, "Oh, I suppose it's not too bad in Palm Beach in the summer, with air conditioning." But it's the heat I like. It slows everything down and makes life easier. The warm nights when you're walking along the beach by yourself are so peaceful. It seems like it's *before* all the trouble came in the world. It's things like that that make me want to stay in Palm Beach in the summer.

Dad and Mom come and go then. They usually stay in Palm Beach through June and then go to France for a month or six weeks. In August they come back for a week or so, and then take off for Scotland or some other cool place until late September or October. Sometimes they split up and go to different places. My sisters, Terry and Beth, spend part of the summer in Palm Beach and the rest in other places. I'm the only who stays the whole summer.

At least that's the way it used to be. But one night a few days after school was out this summer I got the bad news.

Dad and Mom were having a health dinner at

home, and Terry and I ate with them. Beth was in the Bahamas. It wasn't often that there were that many of us together for one meal, and I was a little nervous. Mainly because I was so used to eating alone in the kitchen.

Dad and Mom started talking about what they were going to do during the summer.

"What happens after we leave Cannes?" Mom asked him. "That's what I want to know."

"I've got bigger plans," Dad said. "Maybe I'm not going to Cannes at all."

"You can count me out of those bigger plans," Mom said. "I'm going to be in Cannes."

"Go ahead," Dad said. "It's a free country. But I'm going to Africa."

"Africa!" she hollered. "Africa! Barry, you're out of your mind. Africa in June? You'll burn up."

"I'm going on a special safari, and everyone says it's not all that hot in the East African highlands."

"Who says that?"

"Tommy Shevlin, Bill Holden—people who know."

Mom started to laugh. "We leave Palm Beach to get out of the heat and you go to *Africa*. Barry, you're crazy."

"Have it your way," he said. "I didn't ask you to go with me."

That's the way everyone in my family puts things in the end. If you're rich enough you can always tell everyone else to go do what they want and leave you alone. There's enough money for everyone to take off in his own direction.

"Did I ask her to go?" Dad was asking me.

"Go where?" I asked back in a dumb way. You never want to get between them when they're having it out.

"Weren't you listening?" he asked me, like a threat.

"I heard something about Africa," I said. "And a special safari."

"What's so special about it?" Terry asked. She's sixteen and careless about questions.

"Why do you want to know?" Dad asked her. That's a way he has. He says something mysterious, and then if you ask him a natural question about it, he pretends you're being nosy. But he always tells in the end, the way he did then.

"I never heard of a *special* safari," Terry said.

"They're all special," Mom said. "Close your mouth when you eat lobster."

"Close your mouth when you eat anything," Dad said.

Terry closed it.

"This is a safari to find out something about where elephants go in summer and what they do," Dad said.

"Oh, Barry," Mom said, "you know what they do."

Dad didn't pay any attention to her. "It's not a safari where you kill animals," he told Terry and me. "Except an antelope or so a day for food. It's practically scientific. Some wildlife group is sponsoring it."

Those wildlife groups are very big in Palm Beach now. Especially with the hunters who already have about a hundred heads in their trophy rooms, the way Dad and his friends do.

8

"And I suppose Barry Olmstead is paying for all of it," Mom said.

"I'm paying my share and a little bit more," Dad said, flaring up. "What will happen to the world when all the animals are gone? Don't you think that's a good cause?"

"I didn't know you cared," Mom said.

"I care," Dad said. "I care a lot more than you think I do."

"How much is it going to cost you?" Mom asked him.

"Not as much as you think," he said.

"A hundred?" she asked him, and she meant a hundred thousand, not just a hundred.

"Less than that," he said, but I thought she must be close, from the expression on his face. So did she, because she didn't say any more.

Then Dad got sore. "Why do I have to explain myself, anyhow?" he asked. "It's my money and you all get what you want. You can go to Cannes and Terry can go to . . . where is it?"

"Nepal," Terry said without too much interest.

"Nepal," he repeated. "And Franklin . . . where are you going?"

"I stay here," I said.

"Every summer?" he asked me.

"Sure."

"Why?"

"I like it here."

"But there's no one else here."

"Charles and Rachel and the maids," I told him. Rachel is our cook.

"You mean I keep this place open all summer just for you?"

"Everyone else comes and goes," Mom said.

"*I* won't be coming and going this summer," Dad said. "And I don't see any point in keeping the house open. It's an extravagance." Then he told us how times were tough and we had to economize.

After he finished he looked at me hard. "I can't keep a thirty-eight-room house with six servants open just for you, Franklin."

"I didn't ask you to," I said. "I could stay some place else here for the summer."

"Where?" he asked me.

"I don't know. With the Youmans, the Patricks . . . somewhere like that."

"I won't have you bumming around that way. Acting like a gypsy, like Dale Tifton."

"It's a lot of work to close a house," Mom said. "And then they get damp in this climate."

"You're just lazy," Dad told her.

"That's right," she said. "I'm lazy and you're spending a hundred thousand or so to hold on to some elephants' tails and drink beer with Bill Holden all summer."

"I . . . " he started.

"So we have to economize and close the house," she finished. "What a laugh."

He got mad and called her some names and she

laughed some more and called him Sabu. That was the elephant boy in the old movies. You can still see him on the late show.

Then they had a beauty of a fight and Dad stormed out and Mom was hollering "Sabu! Sabu!" after him and laughing.

Terry and I kept right on eating. If we stopped every time they had a fight we'd look worse than those famine victims in Asia.

The next day I got the bad news. Dad collared me at the pool and I could tell he had a prime hangover and couldn't be argued with.

"Franklin," he said, "you're going to have the best summer you've ever had."

"Where am I going to have it?" I asked him.

"In beautiful Vermont," he said. "Camp Downing."

My stomach turned over and I lost all my self-control. "No, Dad, not a camp. Please."

"Pull yourself together. Boating, swimming, riding. You'll lose all that lard and come back a new man. I mean, a new boy. You'll love it."

I almost fell over. "Not a camp, Dad. I can't stand the outdoors. I can't stand other kids. I hate organized exercise. If you let me stay in Palm Beach I'll lose thirty pounds by myself. I'll live in a room of my own. It'll be cheaper. It . . . "

"Pull yourself together," he said again. "You're acting like a woman."

I was down on my knees by then and played my last card. "Take me to Africa with you."

He actually thought about that and then I could see him decide that I'd interfere with what he had planned.

"You wouldn't like it," he said.

I knew the safari was going to be like any other trip he took, nothing but parties, but I didn't care. "I'll stay out of the way, I'll . . . "

"No!" he said. "That's final. Now get up and face it. You're going to Camp Downing. A lot of kids would give their right arms to be there."

"I'm not a lot of kids. I'm a rich kid from Palm Beach. Rich kids don't fit in at those places."

"Kids from the best families in the East go there," he said. "It's exclusive."

"Nothing is ever exclusive enough," I said.

"You're a snob."

"No, I'm not. That's just the way it is. You know that. You said yourself that . . . "

"*Basta!*" he said. And that was that.

I found out later that he'd only heard about Camp Downing that day. He got the name from one of the McHarry boys. They are called the McHarry boys even though they're in their sixties. Their mother was a famous beauty who owned a lot of racehorses. She always called them her boys even after they were grown, and it stuck. Dad had asked Jack McHarry if he knew a place where Palm Beach kids could go in summer to toughen up, and Jack told him he'd gone to Camp Downing when he was a kid. Terry had been listening to them talk and she told me about it.

"But Jack McHarry must have been there about

fifty years ago," I said. "It probably doesn't even exist now."

"Dad called this afternoon," Terry told me. "It's still there and they have room for you. At first they didn't, but Dad asked them if they couldn't bump someone for a few hundred in the building fund and they agreed. The kid who got bumped was from Chicago."

"He must be the happiest kid in the Far West," I said.

"Chicago is in the Middle West," Terry told me.

"One of those places," I said. I couldn't get over what had happened to me and how fast it had happened. I was so desperate I even asked Terry if I could go to Nepal with her, but she only laughed and said there were already too many boys going.

It's hard to explain why I thought going to camp was such a bad break, but it's got a lot to do with independence. If your family is rich and you live in Palm Beach, you are freer than most kids. No matter how tough your parents are, you're better off. I guess people in the rest of the country used to have a family life, and then maybe the kids out there were better off than Palm Beach kids. *Maybe.* But now there's no family life anywhere, so the important thing is to be where you're comfortable and free. I knew that outside of Palm Beach and a few places like it, people were still pretending that things were what they thought they were once, and that was hard on kids. In Palm Beach everything is more honest. I was sick about going to Vermont, and I wasn't wrong.

2

LATTIMORE, THE SMART KID I met that summer, told
me he read a book once that began with a man saying
the story he was going to tell was the saddest one he
had ever heard. What I ran into when I went up to
Vermont wasn't so sad in the end as it was . . . well,
I still can't put a word to it, but it wasn't sad. It
seemed it at first, but it wasn't.

I had to change planes in New York and my grandmother came out to the airport in her car to shuttle
me around. She lives in Palm Beach, too, but she
always goes north in the summer and usually stays
around New York. She was just a quiet old lady until
my grandfather died, and then she decided to join the
parade. Her hair is dyed orange now and she always
wears pants and drives a convertible.

When she came into the terminal she had on some kind of linen jumpsuit and even in New York people were staring. She was carrying a little stick like a riding crop and the whole outfit made her look like a lion tamer.

"All right, Franklin," she said when she saw me, "let's go."

She's embarrassing, but she's good-hearted under everything and you can't help liking her.

She was driving a special Mercedes convertible, and when she got in she pulled on goggles and driving gloves, even though we were only going a mile or so.

The first thing she said to me in the car was, "Doesn't anyone ever clean you up?"

"I'm not so dirty," I told her.

"You're unbelievable," she said.

When we got to the next terminal she asked me if I needed money.

"I've got some," I told her.

"How much?"

"A hundred."

"That's not enough."

"They'll send more."

"Don't you believe it. They'll forget you. Here, let me give you a few of the higher denominations."

She pulled out a roll as thick as my arm and peeled off ten one-hundred-dollar bills. I took them, but I said, "I don't know, Granma, this is a lot of money for a fifteen-year-old kid to be hauling around. I might get robbed for it."

"Not in Vermont," she said. "Keep it under your

mattress and spend it as you need it."

As things turned out, I did need that money, but of course I didn't know that at the time.

"Buy yourself some clothes," she said. "You look like a refugee from the South Seas."

"All right," I said.

The plane wasn't due to leave for half an hour and we went into the coffee shop at the airport and I had a malted and a few sandwiches and she had a beer.

"You're going to be as big as your grandfather," she said.

"That's what everyone says."

"I still can't believe he made eighty million dollars," she said. "He never seemed that bright. Of course, they say now that you don't have to be bright to make money, but we didn't know that then." She took a long drink of beer. "He started as a bicycle mechanic. Fixing flats in Akron, Ohio, in 1919. I married him in 1920. We lived over the shop. The owner had an extra room up there. Five years later he had his first important patent on tire manufacture and we moved into a big house out near the country club. Now he's dead and . . . well, here we are."

"It must mean something," I said. It was the only thing I could think of to say. Every time I saw her alone she told me that story.

"Don't be too sure," she said, looking at me hard. "It doesn't mean anything to your father."

Then she paid for the snacks and shook hands with me and left. She had her goggles pushed up in her hair and from the rear she looked no more than thirty. Quite a few people were staring at her when she left.

The plane up to Vermont was small, with a propeller. There were only about twenty people on it. We made a few stops before we got to Dexter, the town where I was going. There was a VW bus with *Camp Downing* painted on it waiting out in front of the little airport. I was walking toward it, carrying my suitcase, when someone clapped me on the back and yelled, "Welcome to Camp Downing!"

I almost fell down, and then I turned around and there was a guy about twenty, very brown, with long blond hair. He wore a band around his forehead to hold the hair back. He looked healthy, but his eyes were a little wild.

"My name is Jim Peabody," he said, sticking out his hand.

"I'm Franklin Olmstead," I said, shaking hands with him. I thought it was a bad beginning.

When we got to the bus I saw there was a picture of an Indian looking into space painted next to the *Camp Downing* sign.

We got in the bus and Peabody started talking as we drove off.

"I go to Harvard," he began, "and so that leaves my summers free. I'm very happy about that because it means that I can work here at Camp Downing. Not for the money, but because I was here every year when I was young and Camp Downing did so much for me that I'm grateful to have a chance to pay back at least a part of what I feel I owe the Skipper and the rest of the staff."

That was only the beginning. He went on and on. It was the first time in my life I'd met a New Englander and they love to give speeches like that. I read later some place that they don't like to talk, but that's not true. They talk all the time. And all about life and duty and people they owe things to. You never hear people make speeches like that anywhere else I've ever been, not like they do up there.

Another funny thing about so many people in New England is that they think they know everything, and then you find out they don't know anything. I mean, they pretend like they're modest, but give them ten minutes and they start telling you how everything works. But they always manage to be wrong somewhere.

"When I take my degree from Harvard next year and go to work, I won't be able to come out to the Camp in the summers," Peabody wound up. "It will be a big change in my life." He stopped talking then and gave me a long look from those wild eyes.

"Maybe they'll give you some time off from your job in the summer," I said. He seemed to me to need calming down.

"Three weeks at the most," he said quietly. "That's not enough." He said it like it was a scene in the movies where it's life or death.

I didn't say anything to that and he finally asked me if I was from Florida.

"That's right."

"What part?"

"Palm Beach."

It registered, the way it always does.

"Your father in business there?"

"No."

"I used to know some people named Olmstead from Mystic, Connecticut. Any relation?"

"I don't know. My family isn't much interested in relatives."

"Oh?"

"Dad says that if a relative looks you up it means he's after money."

He laughed and said, "Well, I guess that depends on how much you have."

"We have lots," I told him. I was kind of enjoying myself by that time.

He looked a little confused and then he said, "I can see you're not a New Englander."

I could tell he wanted me to ask how he knew that, but I didn't say anything.

So finally he had to spell it out for me. "In New England, the people who have money never talk about it." I could tell he meant that was the right way.

"Then how do they throw their weight around?" I asked him.

"What do you mean?"

"How do they let poor people know they're rich?"

"I don't know that they do," he said.

"There's no point in having money unless you do," I told him.

That upset him and he said it was ill-bred. Then he

told me the life stories of a lot of rich New Englanders who gave all their money to charity and sent turkeys to poor old women on Thanksgiving. He didn't understand that was just another way of rubbing poor people's noses in it. And more ill-bred than just boasting about how much you have, the way they do in Palm Beach.

After a while I didn't listen to him much, but looked at the country we were going through. It was not bad. It's the best thing about New England, in fact. The land rolls just enough and the trees and meadows and farms are spaced out just right. The villages are clean, and the old houses with the fresh white paint are very pretty. No, the country is all right up there. The problem is the people.

We finally got to Camp Downing. I thought there'd be something built of logs at the entrance, and a big sign, the way you see camps in the ads, but there was nothing. We turned off onto a dirt road that wound through woods for a mile or two, and then we came into an open space, and there it was.

At first, places like that look pretty good. A lake, with cabins built back from it in the trees, boats sailing on the lake, tennis courts, stables, and so on. For a minute I was almost not sorry that I'd come.

"Beautiful, isn't it," Peabody said.

"Uh-huh."

"I'll take you in now to meet the Skipper."

"Couldn't I meet him later?"

"No, it's part of the tradition at Camp Downing

that you meet the Skipper when you arrive. One other thing I should tell you about now. Everyone at Downing except the Skipper is called by his last name. You're Olmstead, I'm Peabody, and that goes for all the boys and instructors. *Except* the Skipper."

"What's he called?"

"Skipper, of course."

"What's his real name?"

"It's not important."

"Aw, tell me."

"It doesn't matter," he said in a sore way. I don't think he knew. I never did find out the Skipper's name, and I don't think anyone else knew it. For a while I thought that maybe he'd been born Skipper, with no real name. But I figured out that was impossible. He'd had a name once, but he'd been the Skipper for so long that it had been lost. That's the way things happen in New England. They get going on something they think is so cute, and before they know it they've gone too far.

We got out of the VW bus and walked over to the administration building. It was made of logs, the way I had imagined.

We went inside and there were a few instructors there, all young like Peabody. They jumped up and threw out their hands and rattled off their names, and I said Olmstead back at them and we all shook hands. I was beginning to feel pretty lousy.

Then the door of the Skipper's office opened and he came out and I felt worse. He was a great big man with thick white hair and always smiling. He rushed over to me and grabbed me and shook hands with me and put his arms around me and told me how happy he was to have me at Camp Downing and what a great time I was going to have. I was standing there feeling worse all the time and thinking how he was what Dad would have called a complete phony. I could hear Dad's voice saying, "Nothing halfway about him."

That's another thing about New England—the phonies are phonier than they are anywhere else. In Palm Beach, for instance, there are plenty of phonies, but there's some point where they stop. In New England, the phonies are phony straight through—they're solid.

I was thinking that if the Skipper hadn't been a complete phony he would have said something that made a little joke about Dad paying him those extra hundreds to bump the kid from Chicago and make room for me. Something like, "It was so generous of your father to contribute to the building fund. Do thank him for me." Even a Palm Beach phony would have been smooth enough to do that. But not the Skipper. He was solid. He couldn't face the fact he'd been bought, so he put on a big show. That's what they call repression, I guess, and they say it can cause a lot of trouble. You see it all over New England.

"Olmstead," he was saying, "here at Downing we usually go one of two ways." He paused and I was really wondering what was coming next. "We are either water types—sailing and canoeing—or horse types. I think you're a horse type."

22

Everyone in the room was thinking that one over.

"I've never ridden," I said. Neither way sounded too good to me.

"My thinking is this-a-way," the Skipper said to Peabody. "In Florida, Olmstead has had his fill of sailing. Ergo, at Downing he deserves a change. Ergo, horses."

Peabody nodded, and so did the rest.

"I never sailed in Florida," I said. "Or anywhere else."

"Never sailed in Florida?" the Skipper asked me. "Never sailed in some of the world's great sailing waters? May I ask why?"

"Never thought of it, I guess."

"But you did go on the water in some form, I trust."

"Sometimes."

"How?"

"Well, we have a boat, and I've been out on that."

"Then you have the feel of the water."

"Our boat is too big to feel anything on it."

"How big?" one of the instructors asked. His name was Coffin.

"A hundred and twenty-six feet. It has a crew of eight and sleeps sixteen. You might just as well be on a liner for all the feeling of the water you get."

They all looked at me for a minute. Then they looked at the Skipper, waiting for him to do something about that boat. I got the feeling it was filling up the room. New Englanders *say* they don't like to talk about money and possessions, but there's nowhere in the world that money and possessions mean more.

"Olmstead," the Skipper said finally, "I think you're

right. You might just as well have been on a liner. Instead of gaining the great experience of the water, you were led tantalizingly close and then . . . you were just too far away."

They all nooded their heads in agreement.

"I guess so," I said.

"You could have the real water experience here at Downing . . . but I still say you're a horse type. And I'm usually right."

"Hear, hear," Coffin said, and they all said, "Hear, hear" after him, and the Skipper waved his hand as though to say he didn't deserve it. That was another tradition at Camp Downing. Every time the Skipper patted himself on the back, all the instructors said, "Hear, hear." It's an expression from Old English and means, "That's right, you've done it again."

3

THAT WAS THE END of the session with the Skipper, and then Peabody took me down to my cabin. It wasn't mine all alone, of course, because there were two other boys in it. Lattimore and Campbell. They weren't there when we went down, but Peabody told me their names.

"They're both very interesting," he said. "You'll like them."

I'd never heard a kid recommended as interesting before. And I wondered if what was interesting to Peabody was going to be interesting to me.

"One last thing," Peabody said. "Do you have any valuables you want locked up? Jewelry? Money?"

"I've only got a hundred with me," I said.

"That's quite a bit," he said in a worried way. "I

think you'd better put most of that in safekeeping. You can draw on it as you need."

"How much do you think I should keep now?" I asked him.

"Suppose you keep ten and give me ninety. That should last you a week or so, and then you can take another ten."

"All right," I said, and forked over ninety.

"I'll give you a receipt later," he said.

"That's all right, I trust you."

"No, no," he said. "We're very businesslike here." You would have thought we were talking about a million dollars or something.

Then he left and I looked for a place to put the thousand my grandmother had given me. I don't know what Peabody would have said if I'd produced that. But I was sure that if I'd given it to him I would have had a hard time getting it back except in ten-dollar bills once a week.

There was a stuffed bird like a hawk over the door, and while I was feeling around up there my hand went in the top through the feathers. There was a hole and it was hollow inside. So I put the thousand in the bird.

The cabin wasn't bad if you like cabins, which I don't. It was made of pine and the beds were at one end, and a table and a few chairs at the other end. Not much furniture, but the idea of a camp is that you're outside so much and so tired by night that you don't care. You just sleep in the cabin.

I lay down on my bed and got ready to take a nap.

It was about five o'clock in the afternoon, and I was pretty tired from all the traveling and meeting the Skipper and the rest. Peabody had told me to take it easy for the rest of the day and start the active life the next morning.

I had just dozed off when there was a lot of noise and I woke up and there were two kids thrashing around with tennis rackets and looking at me. They were Lattimore and Campbell.

Campbell was a thin, nervous-looking kid with pretty bushy hair. He came over and stuck out his hand and said, "Campbell."

I said, "Olmstead," and shook hands with him. You spent a lot of time at Downing doing that.

Lattimore was a normal-looking kid, and pretty big. Not as big as I am, and there was no fat on him.

He just waved at me and said, "Steve Lattimore."

"You're only supposed to use your last name," Campbell told him. "And shake hands."

"Act your age," Lattimore said.

"Franklin Olmstead," I told Lattimore.

"Where are you from?" he asked me.

"Florida."

"What part?"

"Palm Beach."

"Know a kid there named Dale Tifton?"

"He's a friend of mine."

"I met him in Philadelphia last year. He's a wild one, isn't he."

"He's too wild for me," I told Lattimore. "I like him, but he's too wild."

27

"That's about what I thought," Lattimore said.

"I know some wild kids," Campbell said. No one paid any attention to him.

Lattimore and I talked for a while, and then Campbell got sore and went outside.

"He's a mess," Lattimore told me.

"He looks nervous."

"He's a nervous mess. How did you happen to wind up here?"

I told him about Dad and the safari and the rest, and he laughed and said that was pretty funny. "It's a good story," he said, "even if it is on you."

Then he told me he was from Philadelphia. His father is a lawyer there who spends a lot of time sailing. I could see that Lattimore had breeding, the kind you never see much of in Palm Beach. Especially in families like mine. I found out later that the Lattimores have been socialites in Philadelphia for about three hundred years. We've only been up there for about forty. The first thing my grandfather did when he got really rich was pick up a Social Register listing, because that was what everyone did in those days when they made it. But he said later it wasn't worth it. Too easy to get into and the quality was dropping. Dad says the same thing.

Of course, just being a socialite from Colonial days, the way Lattimore was, didn't mean anything all by itself. He had to be the kind of kid he was first—smart and easy to get along with—but then it did sort of add the finishing touches.

I asked him why he was at Downing, and he said it was his mother's idea. His father was off on some ocean-sailing race and hadn't been able to help him.

We sat there feeling sorry for ourselves for a while, and then we started talking about Camp Downing. We agreed that the Skipper was something, and so were the traditions. He told me how to get out of some of the exercises, and I told him I was supposed to be a "horse type."

"That's bad news," he said. "I guess you'll get the same horse Parker had."

"Who's he?"

"The kid from Chicago who was here. He left a couple of days ago, no one knew why. A big break for him, though."

I didn't tell him then that Parker had been bumped for me. I did later, of course, and he found it another one of those good jokes on me. Lattimore had a way of seeing the humor of what happened to me, and I didn't mind because he could make me see it the same way.

At the time I was much more interested in the horse Parker had being bad news, and asked him about that.

"If you're a horse type, you get assigned to a troop," he explained. "And to a horse that's yours for the summer. The horse Parker had is called Klondike and has the shakes. He's hard to stay on and gives you a very rough ride."

"The shakes? Horses don't drink, do they?"

"It's some mysterious disease. He had Parker ga-ga."

I could see then why the Skipper had decided I was a horse type. It was just that he had an extra horse and had to get someone on it. I explained that to Lattimore and he said, "Of course. They never give you the reason for anything around here, but it's always something like that."

The dinner gong rang and we started for the lodge where everyone ate. When we came out of our cabin, he pointed toward a big cabin off at the edge of the woods. It was big enough to be a lodge on its own.

"Stay away from that cabin," he said. "That's where they keep the Connollys."

"Who are they?"

"You've never heard of the Connollys?"

Then I understood he was talking about the political family. "Oh, *those* Connollys."

"They're so rough and there are so many of them that they keep them all together in that special cabin," Lattimore explained. "About twenty of them, I guess. They have their own athletic program and everything. The cabin was built just for them and it even has its own cook and kitchen. Papa Connolly paid the Skipper a fortune to do it, because the Skipper told him they couldn't put Connollys with the regular boys. They even have their own family security guards with them, so they never get out on their own to cause trouble. The only danger is if you go over there yourself. They're like wild lions if anyone gets on their territory."

"I'll remember," I said. "It's the kind of thing the Skipper and the instructors should tell you instead of all that other stuff."

"They like to see a new boy learn the hard way," Lattimore said. "Wander over there and get jumped on. Then they say, 'I guess you'll be more careful next time.' Another thing is that I don't think the Skipper and the rest can figure out a way to tell you in advance, because then they'd have to explain why they have the Connollys in the first place."

"Is there much fighting here? In the rest of the camp, I mean?"

"Oh, sure, but with your size you can take most of them. Although you do look kind of mushy."

"I'm flabby, but I've got a lot of strength under the flab."

"Uh-huh, that's what I thought. You could probably even take a few Connollys, but don't get any ideas, because if one of them gets into something the whole pack piles on."

At the dining lodge there were big tables and benches, and about two hundred kids packed in there, twenty to a table. Everyone had long hair, but only the instructors could have it down to their shoulders. The Skipper sat at the head table with them.

Before you sat down you had to stand silently while the Skipper gave a prayer. It was long, but I was sort of interested because I'd never heard anyone do that before. Of course, after the first time I was as bored as anyone else.

31

When we finally got to it, the food wasn't bad, and there was plenty of it. It was better than the food at our house, to be honest, but our cook, Rachel, is probably the worst in the world. The Olmsteads are famous in Palm Beach for bad food. Rachel can even do something to a catered party where she doesn't touch anything—Dad says she can put a hex on the catering chefs. But she's the only cook we can get to stay because Mom is so hard to get along with.

After dinner there was supposed to be a recreation period in the main lodge for reading or writing letters or playing games like chess and checkers. I didn't do any of those things, so I was wondering where the television was. I asked Lattimore and he told me in a low voice that there was no television at Downing. "You can't harden boys up and have TV, too," he said. "Don't you know that?"

"If you're trying to sound like the Skipper, you're making it," I told him. "But I'm a TV addict—what am I going to do?"

"Don't you ever do anything else at night? Read?"

"No."

"What a barbarian."

It sounded like a tough thing to say, but no matter what Lattimore said to me there was no meanness in it. It was as though he was outside looking at you. And himself. He was what they call impersonal, and so you ended up agreeing with him.

"All right, I'm a barbarian, but it's too late to change now. I'll die without TV. I'm like a fish out of water."

"You'll live," he said. "Mix it up. Meet some of these splendid young men."

"They don't look all that splendid to me."

They didn't, either, but I started talking to a few of them. They all went to Eastern boarding schools like Groton and Hill and Hotchkiss and St. Paul's and Choate during the school year, and they liked to talk about school all summer, too. Lattimore went to St. Paul's and he was the only one who didn't talk about what had happened in the last year there.

One of them asked me where I went to school and I said, "Palm Beach, the private school."

"What's the name of it?"

"It doesn't have a name. It's just called the private school."

"I never heard of a school with no name," this kid said. His name was Swanson, and he was about fifteen, with pimples. He went to Hotchkiss and thought he was great.

"It's like the Skipper," Lattimore said.

"It has no name and no one's ever heard of it," I said. "That's why it's so exclusive."

"I'll bet it's not very high scholastically," Swanson said.

"Of course not," I said. "It's full of kids like me."

He didn't know quite what to make of that. "You admit you're dumb, then?" he asked me.

There was a crowd of them around by that time.

"Sure," I said. "I'm the dumbest kid in the private school in Palm Beach, and you can't get any dumber than that."

"Don't you have any ambition?" another kid asked me.

"Why should I?"

"To do something. To be able to run things in business, or have a profession."

"I can run things anyhow," I said. "I'm rich."

"How rich are you?"

"Rich enough."

"How rich?"

"That would be telling."

We argued around like that and then Swanson got sore and said I wasn't rich at all, and I just laughed. Then he got sorer and said I was the sort of boy they never should let into Camp Downing, and Lattimore and I both laughed.

Then Swanson pushed me in the stomach and I pushed him back and we ended up on the floor with me sitting on him, and when his face got red enough he gave up.

"You're going to be a big hit here, I can see that," Lattimore said when we were walking back to our cabin.

"These guys are all so young for their age," I said. "I thought going to those hard schools was supposed to make you more intelligent, not less."

"Well, no school can compare to that academy of hard knocks called Palm Beach," Lattimore said. "You've seen so much more of the world than these sheltered Easterners."

Later when I told him just how much I had seen,

and about Mom and Dad and all their friends, and how everyone in Palm Beach knows everything is washed up so there's no point in trying to be in business any more, he told me that not one kid in a million gets an education like that.

Just as we got to our cabin a terrific howling started up from the woods.

"I didn't know you had wolves here," I said to Lattimore. "And so close." I was a little scared.

"They sound like wolves, don't they," he said. "But it's the lights-out pillow fight in the Connolly cabin. Only it goes from pillows to chairs and kitchen pots and anything else they can get their hands on. And they like to howl while they fight."

"How long does it last?" The noise was really something by then. It sounded like every Connolly in the world was in on it.

"Their guards give them half an hour. Sometimes it runs over a little, because they can be hard to separate."

Inside our cabin, Campbell was lying on his bed staring at the ceiling.

"I think that Connolly racket is going to drive me mad," he said.

Lattimore just looked at him. And then at me with a smile, where Campbell couldn't see him, as though to say, "Nothing is going to drive him mad. He's that way already." Poor old Campbell, we didn't know how close to the truth that was. Or why, which was even worse.

4

THE NEXT MORNING we had to get up earlier than I'd
ever gotten up in my life. It was six o'clock and I
never would have made it if Lattimore hadn't held me
up while I got dressed.

Then we had half an hour of calisthenics outside
on the wet grass, and I could barely stand. Coffin was
the instructor for our group and after a while he
stopped and came over to where I was.

"Olmstead, you've got to try."

"I am trying, Coffin."

"I don't think you are. You're either flat on the
ground or just standing."

Everyone laughed.

"I've never exercised in my life before," I told him.
"Give me time."

But I didn't get any better.

When that was over we had breakfast and then it was time for the riding. I had to go down to the tack-room and get my outfit. Boots and breeches and some special shirts. They had a hard time fitting me.

When I came out, Lattimore almost fell over. "That's my idea of a cavalry man," he said. "John Wayne rides again, probably for the last time."

We went over to the stables and they were waiting for us.

There were about fifteen in our group. The instructor's name was Greening. The horses were all standing there and Greening said to me, "Here's your horse, Olmstead. His name is Klondike."

I don't like horses to begin with, and have always been careful to stay away from them. On top of that, though, Klondike was a horse that even a horse lover would have avoided. He was brown with black spots and he had dirty white streaks on his face. He was big and had mean eyes, and kept his mouth pulled up from his teeth and his ears laid back. And, of course, he was shaking, like Lattimore had said. Not a lot, just a kind of trembling. I didn't know that was only the beginning. It was after you got on him that the real shakes started.

"Well, I don't know, Greening," I said. "This horse seems to me to have the shakes." I had been planning to say that ever since Lattimore told me about it.

"Horses don't have the shakes," Greening said. "He's just quivering in anticipation. He likes you."

"But I don't like him."

"Why not?"

"I told you, he's got the shakes. And when they have their ears back, they don't like you. And if he doesn't like me, I don't like him."

"Nonsense, it's me he doesn't like, that's why he has his ears back. He likes you a lot."

"Why doesn't he like you? And if he doesn't like you . . . "

"He doesn't like me because I'm keeping him from you. Come on now, let's cut out the conversation and get to it. Up you go."

"I don't know how. I . . . "

But it was no use. Greening grabbed my foot and got it into the stirrup, and he and three of the others got under me and pushed and the next thing I knew I was aboard Klondike.

"The poor old nag never had such a load before," Lattimore said later. "His backbone went down six inches. He almost forgot he had the shakes."

If he did, he soon remembered. Riding him was like sitting on an outboard motor. We started through the woods and he was pretty quiet and I was thinking it wasn't going to be so bad, and then it started. After fifteen minutes I told Greening I couldn't stand it, and he just laughed and said I'd get used to it.

I tried standing straight up in the stirrups to stay away from the vibrations from his back, but that was no good either because then I fell off. By the time we got back I was a wreck.

"I've got to have another horse," I told Greening.

"You suit each other perfectly," he said. "I've never seen Klondike so happy."

Greening was pretty big, and hard to argue with. He had long hair in a ponytail, but he was tough. I was thinking about having a crying fit or something, but I could see it wouldn't do any good.

When we got away from the stables, I told Lattimore I wasn't going to be able to take it.

"That's what Parker said."

"But he got out. I'm stuck. I'll crack up." In the horse program you had to ride twice a day, and I knew I couldn't last.

"Maybe we could get Klondike to crack up first."

"How?"

"I don't know. Give him hoof-and-mouth disease, or something."

"I'll bet he's immune. Anyhow, he's already got the shakes and that's not cracking him up."

When we got to the cabin, Campbell was in a state. He was sitting in a chair with his head on a table and his hands in his hair.

I was looking at him and Lattimore said, "Pay no attention to him. That's all he's after."

"That's not true," Campbell said, picking his head up.

"All right," Lattimore said, "then tell us what's bothering you."

"I can't," Campbell said, and put his head down again.

"That's the answer you get every time you ask him

what the trouble is," Lattimore said to me. "He says he can't tell, but I say there's nothing to tell."

"That's what you think," Campbell said, coming up again. "But if you only knew, if you only knew."

"Knew what?" I asked him. "It can't be so bad that you couldn't tell us."

"It is, though," he said. "If I told, I could get in worse trouble than I'm in now."

"You see?" Lattimore said. "Leave him alone, don't pay any attention to him."

I was too tired to care much anyhow, so I went over and lay on my bed. I didn't even have the energy to get out of my riding clothes. I was thinking that if I was back in Palm Beach, where I belonged, I'd be just getting up.

At eleven o'clock we were supposed to go swimming and so I had to change and go down to the lake. Of course, I'm a rotten swimmer and there were a lot of jokes about a kid from Florida not being able to swim any better than I do. And having practically no suntan.

I thought we were just going to paddle around, but there was a swimming instructor and he got after me and I couldn't rest at all.

Then there was lunch, with another prayer from the Skipper. After lunch we were supposed to have an hour's siesta and I went out like a light. At two we had to get up and go riding again. It was worse than in the morning because my legs were so sore.

Klondike was shaking worse than ever. I kept trying

to make him run into a tree or something and knock himself out, but he was too smart.

We had just turned to come back when there was a noise like a herd of buffalo behind us, and Greening turned around and shouted, "Everyone off the trail!" You could tell by his voice that he meant what he said, and that noise was something, too. Along with the pounding hoofs there was a lot of yelling and whooping. We were on a pretty narrow path in the woods, and it was hard to get the horses off.

We just made it when they swept by us—about twenty kids galloping like wild, with a bunch of men riding behind them, trying to keep up. The kids all had long hair streaming out, and they were yelling and making noises like the Indians make on TV.

It was my first look at the Connollys and their guards, and I didn't need Lattimore to tell me who they were. They had their own stable at Camp Downing and rode any way they pleased, without instructors. Usually at least one fell off on those rides and they had to go back and hunt for him later, then patch him up, or send him to the hospital if he broke anything. The only good thing about the way they rode was that it never lasted for more than a half hour. We had to ride for two hours, so we'd walk and trot in between gallops. But they did nothing except gallop, so the horses couldn't take much of it. They wore out a lot of horses.

"They try to run you down," the kid behind me said. "That's the whole point of riding for them."

41

By the time we got back from that afternoon ride I was gone. I was lying down on Klondike's mane with my arms around his neck. Greening kept telling me to pull myself together, that no one in the history of Camp Downing had ever turned up at the stables in such condition.

"What if the Skipper sees you like that?" he asked me. He was riding next to me and trying to pull me up by the hair.

"I hope he does," I said. "Maybe he'll have pity on me."

"You're hopeless," Greening said.

"You don't know how hopeless," I said. But he didn't hear that because I was talking through the hair on Klondike's mane.

When we stopped I just let go and fell off. Klondike almost stepped on me, but he didn't. If he did that I wouldn't have been around to torture the next day.

I had to lean on Lattimore to get to the cabin. I couldn't make it inside, but collapsed on the little porch.

"Come on, Tarzan," he said. "Time for tennis."

"You have to be kidding."

"I only wish I was."

Changing clothes at that place was almost as bad as the exercise. We had to do it about ten times a day.

I don't know how I got into my tennis shorts and shirt, but I did. I was so far gone by then that even Lattimore didn't make too many jokes. He just said, "Your best outfit, I'd say," and left it at that.

I can't remember the tennis hour. The instructor told me later he thought I was on a drug trip.

Then back to the cabin to change for dinner. It must have been the first time in my life that I was ready to skip a meal. But after I showered and got back to consciousness I made it. I almost fell over during the Skipper's prayer, but recovered after we sat down. As soon as dinner was finished I went back to the cabin and crawled into bed. I didn't even wake up during the Connolly pillow fight.

5

THEY SAY about all those camps that the first day is the worst, and that's true. I don't mean that it ever gets to where you can go through the day without feeling like a dead man at the end, but you get so you don't feel like committing suicide if you had the energy. You toughen up a little, but what really saves you is that you learn some tricks.

You learn how to do the calisthenics without putting much in, and how to loaf around during swimming, and how to fix your tennis racket so the strings are always falling out and you can't play. You get to each thing late and you can have stomach cramps a lot. And Lattimore and I used to have a lot of fake arguments that would eat up time. There are plenty of tricks.

44

The only thing I couldn't do anything about was the riding and old Klondike. He shook worse all the time. I tried everything I could think of, including feeding him tranquilizers in his stall before we started, but nothing worked. I even let him out one night, and chased him about five miles into the woods, but he was back the next morning. There was no way I could get on top of that situation. It was black or white. Either you were on that horse or you weren't. You couldn't be there and not there at the same time, like you could at tennis or swimming or the rest.

The only way I could finally stand to be on Klondike was to ride with my legs straight in the stirrups. That lifted my rear end out of the saddle and the shaking wasn't so bad. But to keep my balance I had to lean forward so my head was just behind his ears. Lattimore called it "the only seat in the world where the rear is higher than the head."

Of course, it made Greening very sore and he was always after me about it. One day he said, "The Skipper saw you riding yesterday and asked me what was wrong. 'Does that poor boy have boils or something?' he wanted to know, and I had to say, 'No, that's his style.' "

"Tell him that's the way we ride in Florida," I said.

"Oh, what a fresh kid," Lattimore said from behind us.

"Who said that?" I yelled.

"I did," Lattimore said. "Want to make something out of it?"

"Wait'll I get off this horse," I said.

"I'm looking forward to it," Lattimore said.

"All right, you two," Greening said. "That'll be enough."

Swanson, the kid I'd had trouble with the first day, was in our troop, and when we got back one day he said to me, "Well, how could anyone named Ox ride a horse anyhow?"

Everyone looked at him kind of puzzled and he said, "In Palm Beach they call him Ox. Ox Olmstead. Because he's so big and fat."

"How do you know that?" some other kid asked him.

"I checked on him," Swanson said. "I wrote to someone I know who goes to Palm Beach in the winter and he asked someone he knows there. He found out that Ox is Olmstead's name. Ask Olmstead yourselves if you don't believe me."

They all looked at me and I said, "Sure, that's my name. I always thought it was kind of nice. Gives you the idea of power. You know, slow but dangerous."

"You're not dangerous," Swanson said.

"You didn't think that when I was sitting on you," I said, and everyone laughed.

"I still say it's funny to see you riding," Swanson said. "How can anyone named Ox ride a horse?" It was the best he could do.

"I think you're right," I said. "I only wish I could get Greening to see it that way."

Swanson went off sore, as usual. I always ended up agreeing with him, and he didn't like that one bit.

"Ox does suit you," Lattimore said later. "Something about the eyes, I think."

"Also the mouth," I told him. "Slow chewing. Watch me at dinner."

"You may look like an ox," Lattimore said, "but you must be the most insolent kid I've ever run into." That was about the highest praise Lattimore could give.

Anyhow, the name Ox caught on around the camp and everyone started using it. It was supposed to be against the rules to call a kid anything except his last name, but Ox suited me so well that even the instructors would forget and use it every so often.

Campbell was getting worse and worse. He had nightmares and howled in his sleep or sat up half the night staring into space. Lattimore was still convinced he was a phony, but I was beginning to wonder.

Finally one day he cracked up completely. It was at night just before we went to bed, and the three of us were sitting in the cabin. Lattimore and I were talking about kids we knew and he asked me, "Who's the worst kid you've ever known?"

"Dale Tifton."

"I don't mean that way. I mean the most boring, the biggest jerk."

"I'll have to think. I've known so many."

So I was thinking, and all of a sudden Campbell jumped up and said, "Come on, say it! It's me you're thinking of!"

"Don't give yourself airs," Lattimore said.

"Oh, I've known a lot worse than you," I said.

47

"You're not so bad. Not as bad as you think you are."

"You fixed this up between you!" Campbell yelled at Lattimore. "You fixed it up so you'd ask him the question and then he'd pretend to think, and then he'd say Campbell. No, I'm wrong. He wouldn't actually say it. He'd start to say it and then he'd stop and smile and you'd smile back and I'd understand that he was thinking of me but he didn't want to hurt my feelings. That's the way it was!"

"You're completely nuts," Lattimore said. "You've got a persecution complex."

"I wish I did," Campbell said. "But I don't *think* I'm persecuted. I *know* I am. And you're one of my persecutors. Admit it! You work for the Schreckers! You work for Granny and Grampy!"

Then he jumped on Lattimore and was clawing at his face and screaming like a girl. I pulled him off and we held him down. His eyes were rolling around in his head and he was twitching all over.

"He's really nuts," Lattimore whispered. "He's having a fit. We better get the doctor."

"I hate to do that," I said. "Once that happens he's a marked man."

So we took turns holding him down.

But he didn't get any better and after about twenty minutes Lattimore said, "He may drop dead or something. We have to get the doctor."

I knew he was right, so he went to get the doctor while I held Campbell.

They came back in a few minutes. The doctor was

named Paulson and was pretty young. I thought that because he was a doctor we were supposed to call him Dr. Paulson instead of Paulson. But I was wrong. You called him by his last name only, just like everyone else at Downing except the Skipper. And me.

"Ah, I was afraid of this," Paulson said when he saw Campbell. He got down on the floor and gave Campbell an injection of something, and in a couple of minutes Campbell relaxed and drifted off to sleep.

"What's his trouble?" Lattimore asked.

"He has . . . delusions," Paulson said.

"He seems under an awful lot of strain," I said.

"I suppose he was saying some pretty wild things," Paulson said.

"He claimed we were persecuting him," Lattimore said, "and that we were working for some people called Schrecker. And also for what sounded like his grandparents."

Paulson shook his head. "What did I tell you? The Schreckers *are* his grandparents, Granny and Grampy, and he lives with them because his parents are dead. You can't imagine nicer people. But Campbell isn't grateful in the least. He says all those crazy things about them, and has delusions of persecution."

"You seem to know a lot about it—his case," Lattimore said.

Paulson looked at him in a sharp way. "Naturally the Schreckers discussed it with me when he first came to Downing. This is his second year here, so we've had other . . . instances. Last summer, after the camp closed, I took Campbell back to Taddington—that's where the Schreckers live, not too far from here—and I had a long talk with them. And also with some friends of mine who live in Taddington. My impression of the Schreckers is very high. Very high, indeed. They are exceptionally warm people. My friends in Taddington confirmed these impressions. The Schreckers are highly thought of there. I'm afraid Campbell's delusions are exactly that—delusions."

"But you say . . . "

"We can't stand here all night, Lattimore," Paulson said. "We have to get Campbell to the infirmary. I think he'll be all right in the morning, but I want to keep an eye on him during the night. You two can help carry him."

The infirmary wasn't far and Campbell wasn't heavy, so we got him up there without much trouble.

After we got Campbell, still sleeping, into bed, Lattimore asked Paulson how we should treat Campbell when he came back.

"Just pay no attention to what happened," Paulson said. "Ignore it."

"What if he brings it up?"

"Still pay no attention. If he gets wild, call me. It's that simple."

"If he's so sick, shouldn't he have psychiatric help?"

"You ask a lot of questions," Paulson said to him.

"I have a right to," Lattimore said. "I have to share a cabin with him."

Paulson thought that over and then said, "All right,

I can tell you that extensive psychiatric help is planned for him this fall. The Schreckers wanted him to have a last summer on his own before that. And there was always the chance that he would recover naturally. But he hasn't, obviously. Anyhow, everything is being taken care of. There's no reason for you and Ox—I mean Olmstead—to worry."

We started out and then Lattimore turned around. "You said at the beginning that Campbell isn't grateful for everything the Schreckers do for him. And then you said he has delusions. Doesn't it have to be one or the other?"

"What do you mean?"

"Well, not being grateful is sane, and having delusions isn't. You can't be both."

"Are you a doctor? A psychiatrist?"

"What are you going to do? Put me in my place or answer my question?"

"You're getting insolent, Lattimore." Paulson was starting to get sore.

"I didn't mean to be. It just seemed a contradiction to me."

"All right, I'll answer you to the best of my ability, but after that no more questions. Campbell is not insane, but he does have periods in which he has delusions. So he can be ungrateful when he is lucid, which is most of the time, and have delusions when he has delusions, which is on occasion. I don't see any contradiction. In fact, the ungratefulness probably leads to the delusions. Now, good night."

51

We walked back and I said, "Ask a fresh question and get a fresh answer."

"There's something about it that doesn't ring," Lattimore said.

"It didn't sound any different to me than anything else in New England," I told him.

"What do you mean?"

"When Paulson was giving us that speech about how swell the Schreckers are, I was thinking to myself that it sounded phony. Like it was rehearsed. If I was in Palm Beach I'd think what you thought—that there's something fishy. But then I remembered that all these people up here talk that way. They are always telling you how nice other people are and how hard they try. So you can never tell what's really fishy and what isn't, because everything sounds that way."

Lattimore just grunted and said, "You're a hard man, Ox."

"Maybe Campbell is really nuts," I said. "And maybe on the other hand he isn't nuts and there's something fishy. But in New England you'll never know which."

"I think New England is as funny as you do," he said. "But I can't go that far. There has to be some sense here somewhere. The thing I think is fishy is that I don't think a guy like Campbell cracks up just like that. He has to have a reason. Something has to be pushing him."

"Why couldn't he crack up on his own?"

"He's too dumb."

We sat out on the porch of the cabin, and I said, "Until tonight you've been saying Campbell is a fake. Now you've gone all the way in the other direction."

"I hadn't seen one of those fits. They're real. But listen, morons like Campbell don't have fits like that unless there's a reason. The only kids who can crack up like that on their own, without being pushed, are kids with something to them."

"Geniuses," I said. "Kids like you."

"That's a very fresh remark," he said. "But you're getting the idea. Say, what are you eating?"

"Chicken."

"Where'd you get it?"

"Off the platter in the dining room—after dinner."

"Where'd you have it? In your pocket?"

"No, I left it in a bag behind the post here."

He looked over in the dark. "It's a whole chicken!"

"You're crazy, just a couple of legs."

"It's a whole chicken!"

"A half a chicken, no more."

"Ox, I give up."

So we turned in, still arguing about the chicken, and forgot about Campbell's trouble.

6

WE WERE REMINDED of it the next day, though, because the Schreckers showed up. We would have been reminded of it anyhow, of course, because we started thinking about it when we got up. And the whole camp was talking about it all day.

But it was the Schreckers who really brought it home. We were getting in from riding when a kid came down to the stables and told everyone that Campbell's grandparents were there. Lattimore and I wanted to have a look at them, so we went up near the infirmary and watched. Their car was parked right in front of the infirmary and they were still unloading Dr. Schrecker, who couldn't walk. I'll explain his trouble later, and also why he was a doctor.

They had to get a wheel chair near his seat and then get him out of the car and into it. It was a job. Mrs. Schrecker wanted to do it all by herself, and she could have, because you could see she had the strength. But the Skipper and Peabody and about eight other instructors were all trying to help, and they ended up pulling in different directions and had a time getting Schrecker settled. Then they pushed him into the infirmary and we all went to our cabins.

We hadn't been close enough to see them clearly. She looked big and mean and he looked shot but mean.

We changed for swimming and went down to the lake and fooled around in the water. A kid named Cabot pretended he was drowning and the instructor made a big thing about rescuing him, and then was sore because Cabot didn't have any water in him when the artificial respiration started. If you're going to pretend to drown, you should swallow at least a quart of water so you can put some out when they start pumping you up and down.

But even so, that used up most of the period and we were in a good mood when we started up to the cabins. When Lattimore and I came into the clearing in front of ours, we saw that something was up. Peabody and Coffin were out on the porch and some kids were standing around staring.

Peabody came off the porch and said, "The Schreckers are inside. They want to meet you."

"I don't want to meet them," Lattimore said. He's

smart, but sometimes he says the first thing that comes into his head. It's because his family is pretty nice to him and he's never had to live by his wits.

Peabody got sorer than I'd ever seen him, and leaned over from the porch and grabbed Lattimore by the shoulder and said, "When the Schreckers *honor* you with a visit, you *appreciate* it. Is that straight?"

It was a tough moment for Lattimore, but he played it right. If he'd said anything against the Schreckers, I think Peabody would have slugged him. But he didn't. He remembered that instructors weren't supposed to push us around physically, so he said, "Take your hand off me." He said it perfectly. Coldly.

Peabody said, "I'll let you go when you agree to be polite to the Schreckers."

Lattimore said, "I'll be polite to the Schreckers when you take your hand off."

So Peabody took his hand off. It was a draw, because Lattimore had to give some ground and so did Peabody. But if Lattimore hadn't played it the way he did, he would have been in trouble. Because the funny thing about rules like not laying hands on kids is that just touching a kid is considered worse than hitting him. I mean, if a kid comes and says, "He touched me," then the head of the camp or the principal or headmaster is shocked and the instructor or teacher gets it. But if the kid gets hit, then the teacher or instructor hauls the bleeding kid in himself and says, "I hit him because I had to," and the head man takes *his* side. That's funny, but it's true. If Peabody had lost his head and slugged Lattimore, it would have been Lattimore who was in trouble. He knew that and he played it accordingly. Of course, if he'd played it perfectly to begin with, he never would have made the remark about not wanting to meet the Schreckers. But even the smartest kids get careless every so often and make mistakes.

Anyhow, after Lattimore and Peabody had worked it out, we went in.

It was a pretty crowded cabin, because Dr. Schrecker in his wheel chair took up most of it, and Mrs. Schrecker and the Skipper were there and they weren't exactly tiny. Then Lattimore and I in our wet bathing suits, and Peabody and Coffin looking in at the door. That cabin wasn't up to such a gathering.

The Skipper stepped forward like a butler and said, "Dr. Schrecker, Mrs. Schrecker, here are Campbell's roommates, Lattimore and Olmstead." Dr. Schrecker stuck out his hand and Mrs. Schrecker did the same and we shook them. It was like being presented to a king and queen at court.

We stepped back and Dr. Schrecker cleared his throat and said, "Boys—Lattimore and Olmstead—I am delighted to meet you. Any friend of Tommy's is a friend of ours. Oh, dear, I should have said Campbell, shouldn't I? I know how seriously you all take the rules at Camp Downing. Well, I apologize. And I hope you accept the apology. Do you?"

He looked around at the Skipper, who gurgled, and then he looked at Peabody and Coffin, and they wiggled all over, like puppies, and said "Hear, hear."

Then he looked at Lattimore and me, and we knew

he wasn't going to budge until he got that apology accepted, which was really only a way of making everyone knuckle to him somehow. So we had to do something and we did the smallest thing we could—we just nodded. He didn't like that too much, but he had to settle for it.

While all that was going on I'd been looking at him pretty carefully, and I knew I'd never seen anyone like him.

His face was wide and very red, and he had thick lips and a thick nose that turned up a little. He was about sixty-five and his hair was white and tumbled around. I learned later that he was in that wheel chair because he had some sort of disease of the nervous system and couldn't walk. He never got any exercise, so he was very fat.

That was what you saw of him, but it was the expression of his face and the sound of his voice and something else that really made the impression. He was a complete phony, of course, but a lot of people are complete phonies, like the Skipper. There was something else. He was all wrong, in a mean way. There was a threat behind everything. You saw the difference between him and the Skipper standing next to him. The Skipper was a joke, but you knew he wasn't going to hurt you. At least he wasn't going to go out of his way to hurt you. Dr. Schrecker was something else. You knew he lived to hurt people.

Then he began talking again. "Boys, I am going to be frank. Last night, Campbell had an unfortunate

attack, and now you know our little family secret."
He looked down at the floor and so did everyone else.
It was like a moment of silence for the secret. Then
he looked up and said, "We hope that Campbell will
recover completely. All of us pray for that constantly.
I pray for it, Mrs. Schrecker prays for it, I think I may
say the Skipper prays for it." The Skipper nodded his
head. Peabody and Coffin didn't look too sure, but Dr.
Schrecker was too smart to give them a look with a
question in it. He knew that guys in their twenties
don't pray for anything.

Then he explained the situation to Lattimore and
me, sounding reasonable but laying down the law.
"We don't know how successful our prayers will be.
Naturally, we do more than pray. We have the very
finest medical help, too. Between the two, the medical
and spiritual, we think we are doing everything possible. We have come here this morning to tell you this,
so you will understand how deeply we all feel about
Campbell and how hard we are trying. We also want
to ask you two—Lattimore and Olmstead—to help in
your own way. When Campbell comes back, you can
be of tremendous assistance if you pretend that nothing at all has happened. If he refers to it, simply
change the subject. Suggest a swim, or a game of tennis. The important thing is that his delusions not be
taken seriously by anyone around him. That is what
the expert opinion advises. And if he has another attack—let us pray that he doesn't, but he may—get Dr.
Paulson as you did last night. I want to thank

you for that. Now, I fear that I have been talking far too long, and I shall cease and desist, just asking at this moment if you are with us, if you will help. Will you?"

"Of course we'll help," Lattimore said. I was a little surprised that he gave in so fast.

"Sure," I said. If Lattimore was so cooperative I decided I had to go the same way. A minute or two later I figured out that Lattimore hadn't said *how* we'd help Campbell, so what he had said was really against them.

Then Mrs. Schrecker started. She was tall and very strong-looking, with enormous powerful hands. You could see she had been good-looking once, but now she was too muscular. She had a funny voice, low and sort of breathless. It kind of hypnotized you. She didn't seem quite as mean as the doctor, but you had a pretty good idea you didn't want to be alone with her.

She leaned at Lattimore and me and said, "Dr. Paulson told us you boys were so interested in Tommy's trouble last night. And asked so many intelligent questions." She stopped and looked at us, but we didn't say anything, so she had to go on. "Of course, an intelligent interest in such a matter is wonderful. Genuine interest is always so much finer in life than indifference, but you don't want to let immature theories of medicine lead you to think you can make judgments about Tommy yourselves."

The Skipper shook his head to show how much he disapproved of that, and Peabody and Coffin worked their lips to give a "Hear, hear," but didn't make any sound.

"Please tell us—reassure Dr. Schrecker and me—that you will work *with* us, that you will not try to help Tommy in ways you think are good, but which may harm him. The only help we know will be good for him is that which his doctors recommend, the attitude Dr. Schrecker has outlined for you. You promised him you'd help. Will you promise me you'll help *only* in that way and in no other?"

It was a tough moment. I could tell Lattimore didn't want to say yes to that, and neither did I, and there was no way to say no.

The only way out was to do something else, so I breathed some air into my nose until it tickled and then gave a tremendous sneeze. It's a trick I worked on a lot a few years ago, and I can always do it.

Lattimore picked it up fast. "Gee, Olmstead," he said, "I hope you're not getting a cold."

"It's nothing," I said.

"Standing there in a wet bathing suit," Lattimore explained to everyone. "Let's just hope it doesn't go into his chest."

I sneezed again.

"Have you ever had pneumonia?" Lattimore asked me.

"Only once," I said. "I fell into the pool at the B & T one night, and the locker room was closed and I couldn't get dried off . . . "

"I didn't realize you boys were in those wet suits," Mrs. Schrecker said. "You must change immediately."

"Just a few sneezes," the Skipper said. He had been

glaring at Lattimore and me all the time we had been batting it back and forth. "All boys sneeze. They . . . "

"No," Mrs. Schrecker said firmly, "they must change."

"They can't change, with us in the cabin," Dr. Schrecker said.

"They can go to another cabin and change," the Skipper said. "Take their dry clothes with them."

"No, we've disturbed the routine of their lives enough," Mrs. Schrecker said with what I guess was supposed to be a gay laugh. "We'll go now."

"They can go behind a curtain," Peabody said.

"No," Dr. Schrecker said. "We're on our way."

Then the Schreckers and the Skipper had a big argument about it, but the Schreckers finally won and left. Of course, it took them a long time to leave. First the doctor pushed his chair onto the porch, and then Peabody and Coffin and Mrs. Schrecker moved him onto a chair while the wheel chair was taken down to the ground. And they carried him down and put him back in it.

The Skipper had shoved us out on the porch to watch all that. When they were ready to push the wheel chair off, Dr. Schrecker waved at us and said, "Good-bye, boys, wonderful to meet you. I'm counting on you."

And Mrs. Schrecker said, "We're both counting on you."

"They're dependable boys," the Skipper said. "You

can count on them." He was standing right behind us, holding each of us by an elbow, and when he said that he gave us a good squeeze. "Say something," he whispered to us.

"Good-bye," Lattimore said. "Have a good trip."

I opened my mouth . . . and then sneezed.

They went off and the Skipper said, "Wave!"

We waved, and finally the Skipper let us go. "Now change your clothes," he said. "And do what you've been told and don't discuss this with the other boys. Aren't they wonderful people?"

"Great," Lattimore said, but the Skipper didn't hear. He was already down the porch steps and running after them. Lattimore added, "So brave."

We went back inside and Lattimore fell on his bed and started to laugh. "I was afraid you were going to have one more sneeze when the Skipper said 'Wave!'" he said. "If you had, I would have broken up."

"I just about broke up myself when he said we were boys you could count on."

Lattimore almost choked. "So did I. The least dependable pair at Downing. The last ones to count on!" And he was off again.

He rolled around like that for a while and then he calmed down and said, "They're the worst I've ever seen. How about you?"

"They're way up there."

"Pure poison, right straight through. Did you see the look she gave you when the sneezing started? She knew it was a fake. She was the only one who was sure. But at the same time she knew there was nothing they could do. So she started insisting we change. I think she's smarter than the mad doctor, even if he is meaner."

I said, "The thing I can't get over is how the Skipper and Peabody and Coffin fall all over them."

"I don't know," Lattimore said. "Money or pull or . . . " He stopped.

"Or what?"

"It's hard to put in words. Some kind of crazy New England thing. Something you can't figure out, something that doesn't have a reason. Or isn't reasonable, I ought to say."

"That doesn't make sense."

"I can't say it right. But it's like England itself. I went there with my family last summer, and I noticed that when you were in a little store in the country or some place like that, once in a while a certain someone would walk in to buy something and all the people in the store would sort of freeze up. They'd go on with what they were doing, but they'd freeze up. And later you'd find that the guy who had walked in was some member of the peerage. It didn't matter if he was only the fourth cousin of a lord, and rundown, and didn't have as much money as the man who owned the store—he had it on them and they all trembled. I think that what the Schreckers have on these New Englanders is something like that."

"With that name?" I asked him. "I thought New Englanders didn't go for German names."

"Well, Schrecker is a social name in some parts of the East," Lattimore said. "And there are Schreckers in banking in New York. And don't forget that in England the people with the most voodoo—the royal family—are German."

"I didn't know that."

"Oh, what an ignorant Palm Beach boy," he said. And then he explained how the Windsors—that's the name of the English royal family—were originally called Saxe-Coburg, after some place in Germany. They changed their name to Windsor in the first World War when everyone was so sore at the Germans.

We chewed around on that for a while, and then Lattimore said, "Social or not, it's a terrible-sounding name, and you have to wonder how anyone can take people named Schrecker seriously. Probably means something frightful in German."

"No wonder Campbell is so shot, living with them."

Lattimore looked disgusted. "Here we've been talking about them when we should have been thinking about him. And all the time before, when I was so sure he was faking. He really *was* in trouble, and I was too dumb to see it. Those two hyenas on his back, it's a wonder the kid has lasted as long as he has."

"But the big question is what happens now? He comes back here to the cabin and what do we do? What does he do?"

We sat and thought about that.

"I don't know," Lattimore said finally. "It looks like the Schreckers have all the cards. If it was just them, maybe we could help Campbell. But they have the Skipper and Paulson and everyone else on their side."

That was the way it seemed to me, too. So we didn't talk about it any more. We just got dressed and went to eat.

7

AFTER DINNER THAT NIGHT I was talking to Russell. He's a black kid who goes to Groton. There were three blacks at Downing and he was one of them. He told me had been in school in some place in Indiana and had made such good grades and everything that his teachers had gotten him to apply for a scholarship to Groton and he made it. For a kid who's supposed to be so intelligent he's not too boring, and we kidded each other pretty often.

Like he said to me that night, "Ox, you should play football. You've got the size."

"I'm chicken," I said. "I don't want to get hurt."

"But think of all the advantages to playing football."

"Name one."

"You could get a scholarship to some university and get a degree in physical education and become a pro player and then a coach. Maybe even a general manager before you're through. It's a future."

"If that's a future I'll take the past."

"Your attitude is negative, Ox."

"I can't get positive, Russell, the wiring is wrong. I'm not hooked up like you guys who get ahead. I'll let you play the football."

"Not me, Ox, I work with my brain." Russell is a little guy.

"You mean you only advise football careers for big fat kids like me?"

"I believe that we should help each other find our destinies," he said.

"If you keep on talking like that, you'll end up running a camp," I told him.

"I'm going into political science," Russell said, "but I suppose they talk that way there, too."

"I'm going to be what I've always been," I said. "Rich."

"That's not a profession," Russell said.

"That's what you think."

Then Swanson horned in, the way he always did when he heard me talking about money.

"Don't trust him, Russell," he said. "He's from Florida and you know how reactionary they are down there."

"I'm not from Florida," I said. "I'm from Palm Beach."

68

"That's even more reactionary!" Swanson said. When he got excited his pimples got redder.

"That's true," I said.

"You see!" Swanson said to Russell. "I told you."

"You're only a theoretical reactionary, aren't you?" Russell asked me. "I mean, you don't actually keep slaves or anything."

"Well, let's say we don't have *many*," I said.

"He doesn't have a whole plantation or anything like that," Russell said to Swanson. "Only a few in the house. He's all right."

Then Swanson got sore, as usual. "You think you're pretty funny, too, don't you?" he said to Russell. "Well, the two of you are *vulgar*. If you were well brought up you'd know you don't brag about how rich you are and you don't make jokes about the position of the black man in the South. You're both *vulgar*."

He walked off like he had put us in our places for good.

"My roommate at Groton is a cretin like that," Russell said. "He drives me bats."

"Well, if you go to those schools, you find out they're full of Swansons. You should have stayed in Indiana, like I stay in Palm Beach."

"There's only one difference, Ox. I'm not rich. I'm poor. I had to go." He was serious then, and his eyes looked sad behind the big glasses he wore.

"Who made you go?"

"My mother and father. They're both schoolteachers and they said it was the opportunity of a lifetime.

They believe in it, and now I have to use words like 'meaningful' and 'enriched' and act as though they make sense to me."

There was nothing I could say to that, so I started talking about Klondike and how I wished he'd hang himself in his stall or something.

Then a kid named Preston came staggering into the lodge with his clothes all torn and bruises everywhere. He'd wandered into the Connolly territory and they'd all come out after him.

We put him on a sofa and Paulson came over from the infirmary and took a look at him and said there was nothing broken. The Skipper gave him a lecture on trespassing, and that was that. No one had any sympathy for him, not one of the instructors or kids.

That night in the cabin I said to Lattimore, "You say I know so much from what I've seen in Palm Beach, but I can tell you I'm getting an education up here. I had no idea what goes on in places like New England."

"Child's play," Lattimore said. "This is a sandpile compared to what you've told me about Palm Beach."

"Yes, they do a lot of tough things there, that's true. But they don't do them just to be doing them. They're always after something. If you get run over in Palm Beach it's because the driver of the car is on his way to a party or to see his girl friend. Here you'd wonder if he wasn't just out cruising around looking for a victim."

"What a mind you have."

"When do you think Campbell will be back?"

"Tomorrow, I guess. I asked Paulson about him to-night and he said he was much better."

Then Lattimore went to sleep and I lay awake for a while, thinking of the club sandwiches at the B & T, and the lobster salad at the Everglades. I wondered if I'd ever get back there. And if the food would taste the same when I did.

8

LATTIMORE WAS RIGHT, Campbell did come back the next day. He was there when we came in from calisthenics, sitting in a chair. He looked a little pale, but seemed a lot calmer.

He said hello and then asked us how things had been. We told him everything was about the same, and then we talked about Preston getting it from the Connollys and Cabot pretending to drown and things like that. We didn't have much time because we were changing to go riding, so it all went pretty fast. We didn't say anything about what had happened to him, and neither did he.

That morning Greening told me my riding was getting worse instead of better.

"That may be," I said, "but I'm getting a lot of exercise out of it. A lot more than if I rode in the regular style."

"How do you figure that?" he asked me sarcastically.

"Everyone else sits, but my legs are straight and I'm always holding my weight up. All of it. I'm getting terrific muscles in my legs. You want to see?"

"No," he said.

We were taking a rest period in a meadow. The horses were all standing around and we were lying in the shade of a tree.

"There they go," some kid said and we looked over to a ridge about a mile away where the Connollys were galloping along. Their long hair was straight out behind them and you could hear the war whoops going.

Another kid said they seemed even noisier than usual, and Lattimore said, "Well, they had Preston for dessert last night, and the good feeling is still there."

There were places on the riding paths where branches grew down close enough to reach them, and some kid was always grabbing one and then letting his horse go on with an empty saddle. It drove Greening crazy when he turned around and saw an empty saddle, but there wasn't much he could do, because the kid would come walking along later and say he'd been knocked off the horse by the branch. No matter how much Greening argued that branches didn't grow *that* low, he couldn't prove it.

I had never pulled that trick myself, because I

didn't see where it got you anything. You had to hang on for a while, which was tiring, and then you had to walk to catch up, which was almost as bad as riding. But the day before, a kid named Adams had told us an idea which was pretty good. Instead of one kid doing it, the whole troop would. I could see something in that, so I agreed. Everyone else did, too. Even Swanson.

When we started off again that day, everyone was ready, and as soon as we were back in the woods and at a good place each of us picked out a branch and swung off. The horses went on, with Greening in front, and when he was out of sight we slipped off the branches. We knew he'd be back before too long, so we piled ourselves up as though there'd been one branch that had cleaned out the whole troop. Two or three kids in one pile, then six, then one tossed to the side, and so on. All unconscious from the disaster.

We were lying there for about ten minutes before Greening came back. He sat on his horse staring at us, and we were all looking at him with our eyes open just a fraction. Some of us groaned a little.

He waited a long time, and then he said, "All right, you think this is pretty funny, but I can tell you it's the lousiest trick that's ever been pulled in my troop. You can all walk in." And he turned his horse around slowly and walked it off down the trail. The rest of the horses had headed for the barn.

I think he was hoping we'd all jump up, but no one did. Most of them didn't because they were sort of scared. But I stayed still because I could see it was a way to get out of the rest of the morning. Maybe the whole day, if we could find somewhere to eat, because you could always say you got lost and couldn't find your way back. I knew there wasn't going to be any punishment for it, because it's too hard to do anything to twenty kids. And Greening would probably get chewed out for leaving us in the woods.

After he was really gone we all got up, and most of the kids started walking back toward the camp as fast as they could go. But Lattimore and I strolled in the opposite direction.

"Let's get lost," I said.

"Let's get good and lost," he said.

We branched off on a side path and found a comfortable patch of grass and lay down. It was peaceful.

"This is the first time I've felt normal since I got here," I told Lattimore.

"I'm happy to hear that," he said.

"Fresh kid," I said.

"I wish I were," he said. "I wish I were the freshest kid in the world."

"Work at it," I said. "Honest effort wins in the end."

"Thank you, Dr. Schrecker," he said, "but I'm afraid it's like blue eyes. You're either born fresh or you can forget it."

That was Lattimore's favorite theory, that I was born fresh and he wasn't.

He kept on talking, but I went to sleep. The grass

was warm and it was a perfect morning for a nap.

I woke up with Lattimore prodding me. "Hey," I said, "I . . . "

"Listen," he said, "I've got an idea."

"Well, tell it to me later. I need some more rest."

"You've been asleep for an hour. You'll get sleeping sickness if you go on that way. Now wake up and listen. It's about Campbell and the Schreckers."

So I sat up and he told me.

"We decided yesterday that the Schreckers have all the cards, plus the Skipper and everyone else on their side. So there's no way we can help Campbell, right?"

"Right."

"But that's looking at it the wrong way. The only person who can help Campbell, is . . . Campbell."

"I must be slow—I don't get it."

"As long as Campbell stays quiet, there's nothing anyone can do. But if he says no, no more Schreckers for me, then we can help him do something to get away from them. He's got to stand up for himself. And with some sense, not just with fits. It's that simple."

"But will he?"

"How do I know that, you Palm Beach simpleton? All we can do is try."

He was standing up then and ready to go, so I got up and we started walking back into camp.

About halfway there, Greening came along with our horses and said, "All the rest of the comedians are back. What happened to you?"

"We got lost in the woods," I said.

"We lost contact with the main body," Lattimore said.

"We were dazed," I said.

"We went in circles," Lattimore said, "just the way they say you do when you're lost."

"Get on these horses before I lose my temper," Greening said.

"Save me!" Lattimore squealed, getting behind me. " 'E's after 'ittin' me, Sir, and Hi hain't done nuffin." He said all that in some kind of lower-class English accent from the days of Dickens in London. He said that was the way they still talk there, but I couldn't believe it. Anyhow, he was proud of being able to do it, whether it was a real imitation or not.

"You frightened him," I told Greening. Then I told Lattimore to pull himself together and get on his horse.

" 'E won't strike me?"

"Of course not."

So we finally mounted up and rode in, with Lattimore cringing away from Greening. And me, of course, with my rear in the air. Greening was very sore, but there wasn't much he could do.

We were late for lunch, but the cook dug us up some stuff and we had enough.

After lunch we were ready to tackle Campbell, but Lattimore was called to the office. We thought it was something to do with teasing Greening, but it was Lattimore's sister and his mother. They were driving to Maine and had stopped to see him.

When I found out who it was, I started for the

cabin, but he said I should come with him and meet them, so I did.

Mrs. Lattimore was a nice woman with breeding. His sister, Anne, had breeding, too, even though she was only about fourteen. She was very good-looking, too.

We were still in riding clothes and hot and dirty. They were both cool and well-dressed, so I felt a little uncomfortable. After Lattimore introduced me, we sat in chairs in the garden near the office.

"Shall I ask you how you like it here?" Lattimore's mother said to him.

"Don't," he said. "I might tell you."

"Oh, dear," Mrs. Lattimore said. "Is it that bad?"

"It's worse."

"Do you agree?" Anne asked me.

"Yes, but I'm not a good person to ask."

"Why?"

"Well, I guess because I probably wouldn't like any camp."

"Oh?"

"Ox has led a sheltered childhood in Palm Beach," Lattimore said. "He has peculiar ideas of personal comfort."

"That sounds interesting," Anne said.

"It's not, though," I told her. "I'm just fat and lazy and Palm Beach suits me."

She smiled at me, and it was a very nice smile.

We talked like that for a while, and then I excused myself and left them.

Campbell was in the cabin and asked me about the riding, and I told him we'd gotten lost. I was wondering whether I should talk to him about standing up for himself, and then I decided that I'd better wait for Lattimore.

Just as I decided that, he brought it up.

"I guess you and Lattimore must be wondering about the other night," he said.

"A little," I said.

"I guess I was pretty wild," he said. "I apologize for jumping on you."

"It wasn't anything," I said. "We were worried about you later, though."

"I suppose Paulson had a long talk with you. And Granny and Grampy—the Schreckers."

"Well, yes, they all talked to us."

He didn't say anything, but looked sort of unhappy and chewed his lower lip.

Finally he said, "I suppose they told you I'm supposed to be nuts."

"Not exactly nuts—upset."

He laughed in a funny way. "Upset . . . *upset*. Boy, who wouldn't be upset after all the . . . after what I've been through. I'll say I'm upset. And probably nuts. But not for the reasons they say."

I was lying on my bed and just let him go on at his own speed.

"It's such a crazy story that no one would believe it," he said after a while. "But it's true. I'm not making it up. I couldn't make it up. You see, after my father and mother were killed I went to live with the Schreckers because Granny—Mrs. Schrecker—is my grandmother. Her husband, my real grandfather, died a long time ago and then she married Dr. Schrecker. He's not my grandfather at all, but I have to call him Grampy. Anyhow, my parents died in a plane crash when I was nine, and I went to live there. I didn't have any choice about where to go because they came and got me. I guess I was glad someone cared enough about me to come and get me.

"And everyone else, all their friends, thought they were taking me because they loved me and all that kind of stuff. So did I, I guess. After I'd been there a year they adopted me. They didn't change my name to Schrecker, they left it at Campbell, but they adopted me. I'm Dr. Schrecker's son, or something. I had to go to court in Taddington and tell the judge how much I loved him and Granny. The judge was a woman, a big one with hair on her face, and she talked baby talk to me even though I was ten. Not baby talk the way you talk to a baby, but with a high voice and little words. She said, 'Do you really love your Grampy and your Granny and do you really want to be theirs, their very own little boy?' I didn't want to say yes, but I had to. I didn't want to, because it was like going against my father and my mother, but the Schreckers were there and I knew there'd be trouble if I didn't. The Schreckers didn't beat me, but they did something that was worse. They'd sit up all night talking and talking and telling me how I did this wrong and that wrong and get me to cry, and then they'd drink and fight with me and each other and I couldn't stand it. So I said yes to the judge—her name was Judge Stella Smith—and now I'm theirs.

"But that isn't the end of it, that's only a beginning. You see, my father was rich. He . . . "

There were footsteps on the porch and Lattimore came in. It was too bad, because I was getting the full story and he was interrupting it. I tried to motion him out with my hand, but he didn't get it.

"Come on, Ox," he said. "I've got permission from the Skipper for both of us to take the rest of the day off. My mother's going to drive us to Dexter and we can spend the afternoon at the club there and have dinner."

At any other time I would have been rolling in happiness. No afternoon riding, no tennis, and then a meal at a club, which meant a steak. I've been practically brought up in clubs, and even a New England club in the boondocks sounded like home. Besides that, Anne Lattimore would be along, and she was a pretty nice girl.

But there was Campbell. I had almost gotten his story, which was what we were after, and I could tell from what I'd already heard that there was a lot more to come. So when Lattimore came in and invited me out for a good afternoon, it meant that Campbell was being left out and he might never talk again.

I knew what I had to do. I told Lattimore afterward that I did it so I could hear the rest of Campbell's story, but the truth is that I didn't care so much about that as I did about the pathetic look on his face.

He was sitting there looking like some poor kid that worked in a factory and was just told that he'd lost his job and wasn't going to have any dinner for the next month.

"Is there room for Campbell, too?" I asked Lattimore, getting off my bed and trying to show him by my face that he was supposed to say yes if he could.

"I don't know," he said.

"There must be," I said. "Cars are so big now. And I'm sure the Skipper would like him to get out of camp for an afternoon, since he's been in the infirmary."

Lattimore had the message then and said, "Sure there's room. And I'll fix it with the Skipper. See you up at the car. And put some clean clothes on, Ox."

"I don't have any."

"Campbell, you look through his stuff. He must have something."

So Campbell and I hunted around and found a shirt and a pair of pants that weren't too bad. With a jacket and loafers I looked all right. I'd gotten a tan by then and my stomach was a lot flatter because of all the exercise.

While we were getting dressed I was thinking that Campbell hadn't really said anything when Lattimore and I were talking to each other about him going. He'd never said he would or he wouldn't. He got dressed, and he seemed cheerful enough, but he didn't say a thing. I think it was because he was so grateful he didn't know what to say.

9

THAT AFTERNOON was certainly the best one I had all summer. It was probably the best I've ever had. Maybe *the* best. We all had some good times later, but that was the first and the best.

Everything just seemed to work out, and everyone got along, and there was just enough of everything, and the food was good.

We went to the Dexter Country Club, which was a lot better than I had thought it was going to be. It was a club for a couple of those counties up there, I guess, so it was organized. We lay around by the pool and talked, and took a walk around the town of Dexter, and then we had dinner, which was almost as good as what you get at the B & T.

Mrs. Lattimore had friends of her own there, so the four of us—Lattimore and Campbell and me and Anne —were able to take off and talk about our own things. I had told Lattimore in the locker room at the club about Campbell starting to open up to me, and how he had interrupted everything. "That's why I invited him," I said. "I figured he'd never talk again if we walked off and left him there."

"Maybe it's better this way," Lattimore said.

"How?"

"He's away from the camp and there are no interruptions. We can get him talking again and he can talk in peace."

"If he'll start again. And then there's your sister and your mother."

"My mother will be with her friends. And Anne . . . well, maybe it's better with Anne here, too."

"I don't see how you figure that."

"You'll see."

Well, he was right, because she was the one who got the whole story, every last detail, out of Campbell. Lattimore talked to her before Campbell and I came out to the pool, and he fixed it up. He told her exactly what to say.

When we came out, the two of them were in the pool and there were quite a lot of other people around. Campbell and I dove in and swam around, too. Because of the swimming lessons I'd been getting I was more at home in the water. I could even swim from one end of the pool to the other a few times. Lattimore was a good swimmer, much better than me, of course, and Campbell wasn't bad. But Anne was in another class. She looked like someone from the Olympics.

We sat by the side of the pool in a quiet place after we got out and had sandwiches, and Lattimore said to Anne, "Have you ever been to Taddington?"

"No," she said, "but I've heard of it."

"How?"

"One of the girls at school has spent a lot of time there—Rosemary Thatcher. She has relatives she visits."

I could see Campbell starting to get interested.

"How does she like it?" Lattimore asked Anne.

"Not too much."

"What are her relatives called?" Campbell asked Anne.

"I can't remember," she said.

"Did she ever mention any people called Schrecker?" Lattimore asked.

"Schrecker . . . " Anne said, thinking hard. "There's something familiar about that name."

"He's a doctor," I said.

"Of course," Anne said. "Rosemary told me the Schreckers were quite spooky. They're old, but they have a boy living with them."

Lattimore gave it a good long pause and then he said, "Campbell is the boy."

She looked at Campbell as though she couldn't believe it, without saying a word. And Campbell nodded his head to show her he was the boy, all right.

"He's got some real problems there," I said to Anne. "He's told us a little about them, and we'd like to hear the rest."

"So would I," Anne said to him. "I hope you will tell us more."

After that you couldn't have stopped Campbell if you'd tried. First he told them everything he'd already told me in the cabin, and then he gave us the rest.

"My father was rich," he said. "He left all his money in trust, in a trust company in Boston. I guess there's about ten million there. It was a trust for my mother if he died first, but they died together so it's in trust for me. I get it when I'm grown up. In the meantime there's an income off it, and some of that goes to the Schreckers to pay for bringing me up, and the rest goes back into the trust fund. But the Schreckers want it all."

"You mean all the income?" Lattimore asked him.

"No, the whole fund. They want it all."

"How do you know that?" Anne asked him.

"I just know it."

"Have you ever heard them say it?"

"No, but I know it. They never say anything straight out, but you can always tell what they want by how they act. It's like the way they work on all their children. It's always got something to do with money and running people. You see, Granny had two other daughters besides my mother, and Grampy had two sons in his first marriage. And her two daughters and his two sons are grown and married and have children. So that's eight married people and more than ten children for them to work on."

"But how do they do this working?" Anne asked him.

"Well, none of those people have any money—I mean capital—and the Schreckers have a lot. So they say to my Aunt Frances, for instance, 'We'll give you a couple of thousand dollars to have Sally's teeth fixed if you'll come up here to Pilgrim's Knob and talk it over.' Pilgrim's Knob is the name of their house in Taddington. Sally is my cousin, about twelve. So my Aunt Frances—this is a thing that actually happened —came up with her husband to Pilgrim's Knob, and that night the Schreckers gave them the worst going-over you ever heard. How Frances was no good, and how Paul—that's her husband—doesn't make enough money, and how they have to help them all the time.

"Frances and Paul are both almost forty years old and the Schreckers talked to them like they were kids. I know, because I heard the noise and listened from the stairs. At first Paul said he made twenty-five thousand a year and worked hard, but they kept telling him he should be doing better than that and that he was a failure. If he wasn't a failure they wouldn't have to be helping him with Sally's teeth. And after a while Paul shut up and then he and Frances just took it.

"The Schreckers drink a lot when they're doing a job like that on people and it ends up in a mess. They scream and spill stuff. But Paul and Frances took it because they wanted the money.

87

"The next day I found Frances crying and I asked her why she put up with it. She said, 'You wouldn't understand.' But I do understand. The only hope Paul and Frances have for money—for capital—is that they'll get some when the Schreckers die. So they think they have to eat anything until then. So do all the other families and their children.

"And the Schreckers never admit what they've done. Frances said that herself. She asked me how I knew what had happened the night before and I said I'd heard the noise. 'They were yelling,' I said. 'You could hear it all the way up in my room.' 'You'd never get them to admit that,' Frances said. 'I told Mother once she'd been tight and shouting the night before and she said, "I never heard such nonsense, Frances, you know I never shout.' "

"Anyhow, that's what I mean about the Schreckers never saying anything straight out, but you know what they want by the way they act. They don't come out and say, 'Let's have Paul and Frances up and kick them around.' They do just the opposite. For a couple of weeks they talk about how brave and sweet Paul and Frances are, and how hard they try even if they don't have any money, and how they deserve help. And then Dr. Schrecker says, 'Let's do something for them.' And Granny says, 'What shall we do?' And he says, 'I have an idea. Let's help them with Sally's teeth.' And she claps her hands and says, 'That would be wonderful.' And they gurgle and talk like that for an hour or so, and I sit there getting sicker and sicker because I know what it really means. What they're really saying is, 'Let's get Paul and Frances up here and kick them around.' "

"Do you think they *know* that?" Lattimore asked him.

Campbell looked as though he didn't understand, and Anne said, "What he means is do they think to themselves, 'Let's kick them around,' or do they really believe what they're saying?"

"I don't know exactly," Campbell said. "They do and they don't. But I can tell you that every time they talk about helping someone they end up kicking him. 'Help' means 'kick.' "

"It's hard to believe people can be that dumb about themselves," I said.

"Don't forget they're New Englanders," Lattimore said.

"What happens at the end?" Anne asked Campbell. "I mean, when all the shouting is over and Paul and Frances are ready to go. Do they get the money? And is everyone speaking normally to everyone again?"

"If they take the kicking they get the money. And when they leave, the Schreckers are falling all over them, and they're falling all over the Schreckers. Everyone is kissing everyone else."

"It sounds lovely," Lattimore said.

"That's why they didn't like my father," Campbell said. "He had money, and he didn't have to ask them for anything. So they couldn't get anything on him and he and my mother didn't come to Pilgrim's Knob very often. They didn't come at all the last few years before they were killed. Something happened between my father and the Schreckers. They won't talk about it, but they drop hints. They say, 'Oh, your father was a wonderful man, of course, but he could be very . . . well, Tommy, he could be very rude on occasion.'"

"That's a pretty good example of Schrecker talk," Lattimore said to Anne.

"I'll bet what happened was that *they* were rude to him and he wouldn't put up with it," I said. "My dad wouldn't take five minutes with people like that. I've seen him with them. He doesn't care what he says to them. Or does."

"What would he do?" Anne asked me.

"Well, he'd never go into a house that belonged to people like the Schreckers to begin with, so it would have to be in a public place like an airplane or something. I guess if he was stuck in an airplane with Dr. Schrecker in the next seat he'd start telling him all about his last safari and then just happen to spill a drink on him. Dad can always figure out a way to give people like that a worse time than they give him."

"He sounds rather frightening," Anne said.

"Well, in a way he is," I said. "He's a playboy. But you never have any trouble with him if you don't get in between him and what he wants to do. He's not interested in being mean to people just to be mean, like the Schreckers. He's only mean when he's crossed. If you remember that, you don't have any trouble with him."

"My father wasn't a playboy," Campbell said, "but he was independent. And the Schreckers can't stand independent people. Anyhow, I can tell they didn't like my father. And they don't like me. They never would have taken me in and adopted me if it wasn't for that ten million dollars down in Boston. They want it. They took me in, and they don't do anything for nothing. The reason has to be the money. And then . . . well, they've done other things."

He put his head down, and we could see he didn't want to talk about it.

"What things?" Anne asked him in a gentle way.

"You wouldn't believe it," he said. "I can hardly believe it myself."

"Tell us," she said. He didn't say anything. "You have to tell someone, sometime, and you won't find anyone more on your side than we are."

"I told someone once," he said, "and it was worse than if I hadn't told anyone. After that I swore I'd never tell anyone again."

"The person you told was already on their side," Anne said.

"How did you know that?" Campbell asked her.

"I didn't. I guessed it. But the difference is that we aren't on their side."

"Maybe you aren't right now, but you can be talked into it. They have ways. And so many friends." All the color had gone out of Campbell's face and he was trembling, even in the hot sun.

"You have to take a chance on us," Anne said. She spoke quietly, but her voice had a lot of strength in it. It was reaching through all his fear to him.

When he turned to look at us his lips were twisted up, but his eyes were steady.

"All right," he said. "They're trying to drive me crazy."

The minute he said it I believed him. So did Lattimore and Anne, and I guess Campbell saw that. We didn't say anything, but he must have seen it, because he went on.

"It started right after I got to Pilgrim's Knob. They treated me like I wasn't quite all there. I'd forget where my schoolbooks were, or something like that, and they'd look at each other and get a worried expression on their faces, and say, 'Of course the books don't matter, Tommy, but you lose so *many* things.' I was only nine or ten then, so I had to blurt out everything I thought, and I'd say, 'But I don't.' And then they'd start listing the things I had lost in the last month or so. A pair of tennis shoes, and a compass, and so on. And Grampy—Dr. Schrecker—would say, 'We're worried about you, Tommy.' And he'd be close to me, holding me by the hand and talking to me in a fake gentle way, and I'd be frightened.

"I couldn't tell you all the things they did like that. I was always doing something wrong and they were always being so fair about it and so worried about me.

"You see, in the beginning I believed them. I thought I really was losing things all the time and making all kinds of other mistakes. But after a while

I began to wonder. I didn't really suspect them then, I just began to wonder.

"One day Granny had a big argument on the telephone with Peggy—that's my other aunt—and I heard it, and afterward I said something about her having an argument. I said it just as a little joke, because you could hear her all over the house. But she said, 'What argument? I wasn't having an argument.' 'I could hear you,' I said. 'You were talking very loud.' 'I was not,' she said. 'You must be imagining things.' It was the same thing Frances had told me about.

"That night she told Grampy that I had accused her of yelling on the telephone and that I was imagining things. Then the two of them started in on me, telling me over and over again that I was inventing things I hadn't heard. They were slow and quiet and didn't drink, and it went on for hours. At the end they almost had me convinced. I began to think I had imagined her yelling. So when they finally said, 'Now do you agree? Do you see how you've been inventing things?'—I said, 'I guess so.' It was the first time I'd given in like that.

"But later, in the night, I knew I had heard her the way I had known at first, and that I hadn't been imagining things. Then I had to try to figure out if she knew she was lying, or if she really believed it. And I couldn't figure that out. I still can't."

I could hear Lattimore suck in his breath, but he didn't say anything. I knew he wanted to say, "Of course they knew what they were doing!" But he didn't say anything because he didn't want to interrupt Campbell. None of us did.

"From then on," Campbell said, "I was better off in one way and worse in another. I was better off because I knew they were working on me, and I was worse off because knowing that was . . . well, it was hard to know it. And not to be able to figure out if they knew what they were doing or not. There was another thing, too. Once I admitted I had imagined one thing, the way I did that night, they had me. From then on, they could always say I had invented something else, and if I denied it they always reminded me of the first time. So they'd get me to admit the new one, and every time I did that they had that much more control.

"I was scared by then. I knew they were after me and I was afraid of what would happen if I denied inventing and they really turned on me. I didn't have any friends, and no one to talk to, and I knew I couldn't stand up to them all by myself. My only chance was to keep agreeing and hope for a break."

Anne looked at me, and I could tell she was thinking that all this had happened to him when he was only eleven or twelve years old.

Campbell saw the look and must have had an idea of what it meant, because he said, "It was bad, but it wasn't as completely bad as it sounds. Things like that don't go on for twenty-four hours a day, you know. If they had I wouldn't be here. There'd be maybe one or two a month, and they only lasted a few hours. They worried me a lot, but I did get to go to school and I did see other kids. I didn't worry about it all the time, the way I do now. And the Schreckers didn't have the time to work on me every minute. They had a lot of other people to think about. It was bad then, it was terrible, but it wasn't too much."

He looked up at the sky, thinking. Just past the big bush of hair he had, I could see the adults at the other end of the pool talking and laughing, and I wondered what they'd say if someone asked them what *we* were talking about. Sports? Sex? Drugs? The sun was so bright and it was such a nice summer day—I'd bet my life they never would have thought of a story like the one Campbell was telling us.

Then he went on. "It got worse after the first time we went into Boston to see Dr. Foster and the trust manager. That was last year. One day Granny and Grampy got me in his study for a conference and she said, 'Tommy, we're going to Boston the day after tomorrow to take you to see Mr. Hugo Lewis, who's the head of the trust department at the New England Exchange Bank.' Then Grampy said, 'You've never met Mr. Lewis, and he's a very nice man and he feels, and so do we, that you should meet each other. After all, he's responsible for managing your father's money.' They didn't say anything about Dr. Foster.

"So we went down to Boston—Grampy could still get around on crutches then—and in to see Mr. Lewis. He seemed all right, and he took me around the bank. He asked me how I liked Taddington and questions like that. Then I waited outside his office while he talked to Granny and Grampy. They were with him a long time. When they came out, he seemed sort of worried and stared at me a few times. They weren't saying anything except good-bye, but they were all looking hard at each other.

"When we left the bank, Grampy said, 'I know someone Tommy would like to meet—Ward Foster.' 'Oh, he would,' Granny said. 'Why don't we go by Ward's?' I thought they were talking about a man's house, but when we got out in Cambridge we went to a big medical building. He's connected to Harvard. Of course, when I saw the office and his name on the plate saying he was a psychiatrist, I knew they had planned the whole thing. The only real surprise was that Dr. Foster was so nice. He was about thirty-five, and I liked him right away. He took me into his private office and the Schreckers went off to do some errands and said they'd be back later. You can see how it was planned. Dr. Foster is a busy man, and he couldn't have had a couple of hours for me by accident.

"He talked to me about skiing and a lot of other things, and I could tell he was really interested. It wasn't just the words. And even after what happened, I still know he's a nice man. Whatever he did—and whatever he's still going to do—he honestly thinks he's doing the right thing. Anyhow, we talked, and after a while he said how lucky I was to live with Granny and Grampy. He said it, but there was a question in it, too. He was looking at me when he said it, and I could see he was all right, and so I fell apart. I'd been holding myself together for so many years, you have to remember, and here was the first person who ever seemed like someone I could talk to. And tell what was happening up there. I knew it had all been planned, but I didn't hold that against him, because he thought he was really helping. And even if it had been planned, I suppose I thought that once he *knew*, he'd be on my side.

"Of course, I didn't start talking all at once. I had to cry first. I broke down and cried and threw up. He took care of me all through that, and then I lay down on a cot in his office and I told him everything. I told him what I'm telling you. The only trouble was that I didn't tell it right. I didn't tell it so *he* could see it. I just spilled it out. I was pretty hysterical, and it all came in bits and pieces.

"Even if I'd told it right, though, I don't think he would have believed it. It all turned on the Schreckers being as bad as they are, and he couldn't swallow that. A grown-up just can't believe that respectable people can be the way they are.

"Dr. Foster would ask me things like, 'Why would the Schreckers want your money, Tommy? They have plenty of their own.' And I'd say, 'I don't know why. All I know is that they do.' He was always wondering *why* they would do this and that instead of wondering why *I* was there telling him a story like that. It was easier for him to believe that a kid would invent the whole thing than that they were bad. So he believed what was easier. He never stopped being nice, but he took the easy way. How can you blame him? They all do.

"At the end I could tell he had done that, and I knew I'd ruined myself. I got off the cot and made one last try. I got down on my knees and cried again and begged him to believe what I had told him and not send me back to the Schreckers. But it didn't work. He just patted my head, and then he gave me an injection and it put me to sleep and the next thing I knew, I was waking up and the Schreckers were taking me out of the office. Dr. Foster shook hands with me and smiled and said he hoped we'd meet again. I knew afterward that they'd all talked when I was asleep and figured out the program. He had advised them to give me a year to see whether I could get over my delusions without treatment. If I couldn't, then he'd take me as a patient at his Boston clinic in the fall. He runs it for kids who have trouble.

"So now the year has passed, and I'm no better. I have more attacks, not less. So I'll have to start with him in the fall. I suppose Granny will take me down. And after a while I'll go from his clinic into a real sanitarium, and then they'll get all my money."

Lattimore started to say something, but Campbell went on.

"The Schreckers didn't mind waiting for a year after they had Dr. Foster with them. Because once he agreed with them that I have delusions they couldn't lose. They were able to tell the school and everyone they knew that I was sick in the head. They had me ringed and there was nothing I could do. All they had to do was sit back and wait. If they drove me nuts, really nuts, then I'd have real breakdowns and they'd be proved right that way. If they didn't drive me nuts, the tension was still going to be too much and I'd blow up every so often, like I do, and they'd be right that way. I try not to blow up, but I can't help it every once in a while. I don't kid myself that living the way I have hasn't made me a little nuts anyhow. I know that. So if the Schreckers don't get me one way, they will another."

He stopped then.

"Unless you do something," Lattimore said.

"What can I do?"

"Isn't there someone you can go to? Your father's family?"

"They're all dead."

"One of your mother's sisters?"

"They'll always go along with the Schreckers. They need money from them because they've never had any themselves. They'd chop off their own kids' heads if the Schreckers told them to. Anything to keep those hand-outs coming in, and to have a chance to inherit when the Schreckers finally die."

We thought that over and then Lattimore asked him if there wasn't some lawyer or professional person in Taddington who'd stand up for him. Someone who knew the Schreckers and saw them for what they were.

"You don't know Taddington," Campbell said. "There's no one there who doesn't fall all over the Schreckers. Oh, I've heard of a few people who aren't wild about them—one old woman in particular, some

99

crazy old actress, I can't think of her name—but they don't have any influence. No, if I couldn't get through to Dr. Foster I'm not going to get through to anyone."

"You could run away," I said.

"I'm not that tough. Besides, you know I'd get caught and brought back. The only kids who can run away are poor kids. The Schreckers would have every policeman in the country looking for me."

"Can't you just let go?" I asked him. "Cry and slobber and make a mess out of everything? That's what I'd do."

"They'd just call me nuttier," Campbell said.

No one said anything.

Then he said, "I began to think that I'd let them have the money if they'd let go of me. But there's no way to say that. And then I thought that after they finally get me into a sanitarium and have the money, I'd be free. But I'm afraid of that, because I'd probably be so crazy, really crazy, by then that I couldn't come back. Or they wouldn't allow the doctors to let me out, anyhow."

Lattimore and I looked at each other. We were the ones who had said that if Campbell would stand up for himself we could help him. But there was more to it than we had thought. It looked as though he was so ringed in, as he said, that it didn't matter what he tried to do.

"We've got to get some adult," Lattimore said, almost to himself.

"How about Mother?" Anne asked him.

"Don't get your family into this," Campbell said.

"She'd do something, I guess," Lattimore said. "But it sounds to me as if they're dug in pretty deep up here, and I don't think her connections are that strong in Vermont. My father's aren't, either. And it would be bad to try and lose, because there might not be a second chance. It has to be someone you know from the beginning is stronger than they are, someone who can't lose."

"That's another thing," Campbell said. "They like people to fight them."

"What do you mean?" Anne asked him.

"Last year, for instance, some of Grampy's relatives were fighting with him over some trust fund they and Grampy have together. They live out in California and the fund was set up in Taddington. So they had to get a lawyer in Taddington to represent them. But the whole town is for the Schreckers, so any lawyer those relatives got was going to really be for the Schreckers. They finally picked a lawyer named Allen and he ran right to the Schreckers. He and the Schreckers' lawyer and the president of the bank came up to a meeting at Pilgrim's Knob, and all the whole bunch of them did was laugh, because Allen was only going to pretend to the people from California that he was on their side. It was all fixed. When the people from California finally figured that out, they got a lawyer from somewhere else in Vermont—Montpelier, I think—and the same thing happened to him. It was all fixed because the Schreckers knew people who knew him and so on. Those people could have gotten the governor himself for their lawyer and it wouldn't have done them any good. The Schreckers can fix anyone in Vermont."

"But they don't think of themselves as fixing things," Anne said.

"You're right," Campbell said. "Of course they aren't fixing anything, they're respectable people. They were just reminding their friends of that. And the friends weren't being fixed. They were just having a laugh at how impossible it was for nasty people from California to cause the lovely Schreckers trouble as long as the Schreckers had such good friends. The friends weren't being fixed, they were King Arthur's Knights rescuing people in distress, the Schreckers. In the end, after the people from California gave up, the only thing that had really happened was that the Schreckers were stronger than ever. That's why they like a fight, because it gives them a chance to run around and jump up and down and get everyone in Taddington excited and more in their power."

He said all that so calmly that you knew he was telling the truth.

Lattimore didn't say anything more. For the first time since I'd met him he didn't have the answer. We were all sitting there without saying anything. I don't know how long we would have been like that if Anne hadn't done something.

"Let's have a swim," she said.

We all looked at her, and she went on. "Look, this is too much to take in all at once. I wish we could come up with an idea right now that would work, but we can't. We're going to have to let it all sink in before we can even start to figure it out. If you want my opinion, we should enjoy the rest of the day and not talk about it any more. Not even think about it, or think about it as little as we can. Tomorrow, Mother and I are driving on to Maine, and I'll be thinking then as hard as you will. As soon as one of us gets an idea we can telephone each other. That doesn't sound like much," and when she said that she was looking straight at Campbell, "but it's all we can do now. It's better to do it that way than rush in without a plan. I know it seems like nothing to you, but trust us. We won't let you end up in a clinic in Boston. Everything will be all right. You'll see."

She sounded good, but no one really believed it. I didn't think she believed it herself. We all *hoped* we could do something, but hoping is different from being sure.

I suppose Campbell knew that, too, but he'd had no friends for such a long time that he was almost cheerful, even if he was going down the drain. Having some friends was more important to him than what was coming.

You could tell by the way he looked at her and Lattimore and me and said, "I trust you." He didn't mean he trusted us to get anything done. He meant he liked us and he was grateful we were his friends. It was sort of pathetic, and made you realize even more than anything he'd told us what a time he'd had.

10

WE DID DROP IT for the rest of the day. Even Campbell did, because he was so happy to have some friends.

We swam around for a while, and then we got dressed and took a walk around Dexter. We talked to Anne about Downing, and she laughed at those stories, and then she told us what she'd been doing that summer. She called it "just the usual Philadelphia things," but she made it sound interesting. I've never met a girl who can talk the way she can. In Palm Beach the girls don't open their mouths except to ask for something or tell you what they don't like or how much money their parents have. You never meet a girl like Anne in Palm Beach. Even Natalie Gregg, who does have some breeding and used to be pretty pulled together, has started to fall apart since we were in the fourth grade together.

Then we walked back to the club and found Mrs. Lattimore and had dinner. I had a steak and so did Campbell. Anne had lamb chops and Lattimore and his mother had some sort of curry. My steak was a big one, and I tried to go slow on it, but I still put it away pretty fast and when I looked up everyone was grinning at me.

"How about another one of those?" Mrs. Lattimore asked me.

"You'd better order two," Lattimore said. "That was only an hors d'oeuvre for Ox."

"One more will be enough," I said, because I didn't want to be a pig, and I must have said it pretty seriously because everyone laughed again.

By the time I had eaten the second one, with another baked potato and salad, I was feeling pretty normal. While I was eating, Lattimore was telling the rest of them stories about Camp Downing. And about me. I didn't mind, because they were pretty funny. When he told Mrs. Lattimore how I rode Klondike she almost choked.

"It's too much," she said when she got her breath. "You'll have to stop."

"The thing that's so wonderful about Ox is that he doesn't get anything about the East," Lattimore said. "It's all built on little details of dress and speech and behavior and other snobbisms, and he doesn't get a one. They could stand that if he were a farmer or something, but with all that Olmstead money behind him it's too much. Huck Finn comes to Beacon Hill with the usual bare feet, but they're sticking out of a Rolls-Royce."

"You don't need so many shoes in Palm Beach," I said, and Lattimore said, "See what I mean?" and they all laughed again.

They started asking me questions about Palm Beach and I told them a little about how my family lived. Not anything too much, just the little things. Then Mrs. Lattimore asked me how I got to Downing, and I told her about Dad's safari and how that had turned into Downing for me. No one said anything when I finished.

"Well, I'm responsible for you being here," Mrs. Lattimore finally said to Lattimore, "and I don't know whether to apologize or not. It's so hard for a woman to know about camps," she said to all of us. "And the place was recommended by friends. I felt terrible earlier today about putting a son there—after the way you boys talked about it—but the more I hear the more I wonder if it isn't a good thing after all. Where else could you have had such a circus? The Skipper and the Connollys and all the rest. I'm not a bit sorry now. I envy you. It's an experience you'll treasure, if not quite in the way the brochure claims."

"You're twisting it around," Lattimore said.

"It sounds funny when you talk about it," I said, "but it's pretty awful when you're there all the time."

"Where else would you have met Ox?" Anne asked Lattimore.

106

"Well, I give you that point," Lattimore said with a grin. "I don't know whether it's worth a full summer at Camp Downing, but it does take some of the taste out."

We kidded around like that for a while and then we went to a carnival that was outside Dexter. There were rides and shooting galleries and all that stuff, and we did everything. We even ate cotton candy. While the rest of them went on some ride that looked too hard on the stomach to me, Anne and I went on the Ferris wheel.

"The Ferris wheel is pretty tame," I told her.

"It's nice, though," she said. "Nicer than those things that turn you inside out."

When we started up she put her head against my shoulder. "You're comfortable, Ox," she said. "You're so solid."

"It's not muscle," I said. "It's fat."

"Whatever it is, it makes you seem solid. Dependable, older." She straightened up and looked at me. "Anyone with two steaks in him just has to be easy to be with."

She was kidding me in one way, but in another way she meant it. She was like her brother. They had everything, but it was as though they'd never met anyone they could relax with. They were both too smart for most kids. Most kids don't like intelligence in another kid, but I do. I was as relaxed with them as they were with me.

She was looking at me, and the lights from the carnival way below us were going across her face in the dark. It made her even prettier.

"Oh, I'm easy to be with," I said. I was thinking that she was, too, and I was sure she knew I thought so because she leaned back again and we didn't say much of anything for the rest of the ride.

When we got down she said, "I'll call, after Mother and I get to Maine. My brother has our telephone number and I have the one at the camp. One way or the other we'll do something about Tommy."

"Yes," I said.

"So I won't say good-bye now. We'll probably see each other before the summer is over, before you go back."

"I hope so."

"If we don't, you might come to Philadelphia sometime. My brother told me he'd asked you."

"I'd like to come. But I'd have to get winter clothes and fly up, and my family is really something about handing out money to kids."

"We'll loan you some," she said.

"I was kidding," I said. "I could get the money. And I'd like to come."

"I know you were kidding," she said.

"I wish I could ask you and Lattimore to Palm Beach, but my family is too much. And they'd never let me have guests. This time I'm not kidding."

"I know," she said. "I can tell the difference."

Then we had to start back to camp to make the curfew. Mrs. Lattimore drove us. No one said much on the way. We had had too good a time, and it was like going back to jail.

When we got out, Campbell and I thanked Mrs. Lattimore and said good-bye to Anne. Anne and I just said good-bye and you wouldn't have known we'd already gone through it at the carnival. When Anne said good-bye to Campbell she smiled at him without saying anything more, but it was enough. She told him in the way she smiled that she wouldn't forget his problem.

At the end we all sort of talked at once and then they drove off and we walked down to the cabin. We were tired, but we were too keyed up to sleep, and now that we were alone we couldn't help going back to Campbell and his trouble. So we lay awake in the dark and talked about it.

"You say the Schreckers have a lot," I said, "but they still want yours. That's what the doctor in Boston wondered about and that's what gets me, too. Why?"

"I don't know," Campbell said. "Some people are just like that. No matter what they have, they want more."

"Maybe the Schreckers don't have so much after all," I said. "How much would you guess?"

"I don't know," he said. Like most of those Eastern kids he froze up when you asked him for a figure.

"Well, guess. One mill? Five?"

"Mill? Oh, you mean million. I'd say they have at least a couple of million in capital. But it's all tied up in trust funds they inherited and . . . got other places. They only get the income."

"They only have a couple of million?" I said. "You can hardly get into the Everglades with that. And only the income off it? Why, that's only . . . " I started to figure it out.

"At six percent, that's a hundred and twenty thousand a year," Lattimore said. "A pretty good income."

"And Grampy makes a lot, too," Campbell said. "But they pay a lot of taxes. So they're always looking for deductions."

"What does he actually do?" Lattimore asked him.

"He's some kind of a research expert on cancer," Campbell said. "Until he had to get into the wheel chair for good about six months ago, he had his own lab and everything at Sturgess. That's about forty miles from Taddington, where they have the university. He used to drive over there every day. The lab was set up on a big grant from some foundation. He had over twenty people working for him. They paid him sixty thousand a year to run it. He's a famous man in his field and he's published lots of books."

"But now he's out of it?" I asked Campbell.

"About halfway out. He only goes over two or three times a week. But he still does a lot of writing at Pilgrim's Knob."

"If he's such a big research expert, why is he so interested in money?" I asked.

"I'll answer that one, teacher," Lattimore said. "Everyone with any money, except you all-out billionaires in Palm Beach, is tied up in this trust-fund business. Their job is only a cover. They have to look as though they're working to keep their money, especially when they're young, because then their parents are still alive and can cut them out if they're lazy and don't work. So they start working for effect and get the habit. Because usually their parents don't drop dead until their kids are old themselves."

"That's right," Campbell said. "Grampy was fifty-five when his mother finally died and he got that trust fund for keeps. Up until then she could cut him out of it any time he rubbed her the wrong way."

"The thing to remember is that they're always thinking about the trust fund," Lattimore said. "They never talk about it, but that's all they're thinking about. The job is just a blind."

"How do you know all about that?" I asked him.

"My father is a lawyer," he said.

"But in Philadelphia," I said. "Not in New England."

"The trust-fund game goes on all over the country," he said. "It's bigger up here, but it goes on everywhere. My father says it's all anyone ever thinks about —anywhere in America."

"You're right," Campbell said. "So is your father."

"I'm getting an education," I said.

"I was waiting for you to say they don't think that hard about trust funds in Palm Beach," Lattimore said.

"They don't," I said. "They think some, but not all the time. If they did, they couldn't enjoy themselves."

"Yes," said Lattimore, "but as I keep telling you, the people in Palm Beach and a few places like that are the people who don't need to worry about a front and never did. They had their money when they were young, and didn't have to impress some mother or trust officer. And, of course, their money was so new that they didn't have that Eastern tradition of working even if you're rich."

"You've got it all figured out," I said. "There are plenty of trust-fund waiters in Palm Beach, but most of the Old Guard have always had their own money, so even the waiters feel a different atmosphere. And there are no jobs, so not even the biggest waiters can put that act on."

"Let me tell you how far the money thing goes with people like the Schreckers," Campbell said. "Do you know that one reason they adopted me was because that made me a Vermonter, and if I was a Vermonter they wouldn't have to pay the out-of-state fee to have me in the Taddington Public School?"

"I thought they adopted you because they wanted to get at the big fund," I said.

"They did, but saving that fee was a little bonus. I know, because I heard them talking about it with some lawyer a few months ago."

"How much was the fee?" I asked him.

"About four hundred dollars," he said.

"It's hard to believe," Lattimore said.

"Everything about them is hard to believe," Campbell said.

Lattimore and I didn't say anything to that. What could we say?

Then Lattimore said, "It isn't the money games that interest me, but whether the Schreckers are bats or not. You keep saying they don't know what they're doing, but they *have* to know. Or if they don't know, then they're completely nuts."

"I can't decide," Campbell said. "Sometimes I think they're one thing one minute and another the next."

"Crooks when they're sane, you mean, and maniacs when they're nuts?"

"Something like that."

Lattimore didn't say anything to that, either. It was like the money—what could we say?

Then Campbell told us some more strange things about the Schreckers. How religious they were, and how Dr. Schrecker said Mrs. Schrecker was a saint because she was so good to people. Only he didn't call her a saint, he said she was "a religious." And how he had written a book for his grandchildren called *The Way*, all about how good life was if you were kind and sincere. And how they loved art and music and plays and everything cultural. And how they knew all kinds of artistic people and were always having them to Pilgrim's Knob along with the scientific people and the bishops and how wonderful everyone thought that was, mixing up such different groups. The Schreckers were famous, and everyone said it was only fair because they were so intelligent as well as kind and sincere.

Lattimore couldn't get enough of that talk, but it had me spinning and I said I had to have some sleep.

Then Campbell stopped talking and we all drifted off.

But before I went to sleep I was thinking that the real trouble was that they all had the wrong idea of what a lot of money was. Everyone kept saying the Schreckers had a lot, but all they had was two million. That sounds like a lot to poor people, but when you're really rich it's peanuts. Dad and his friends pay wives that much in one check when they divorce them, wives they meet on an airplane or some place and divorce a year later. They put out that much on racing stables in a single year, or blow it on one boat. So two million isn't much, but up in New England they fall all over themselves about it. Why, Dad's got sixty or seventy million and he doesn't think that's so much. I mean, he doesn't think he's as rich as people like the Parrys or the Bristows, people with two or three hundred million. Or really, really rich people like Howard Hughes or J. Paul Getty, with a couple of billion each. So how can everyone say the Schreckers have a lot, I asked myself. I still think it was where a lot of the trouble came from.

And another funny thing about people in New England and money is that they get the person and his money all mixed up. I mean, Dad could bump that Parker kid for me because his money was as good as any Chicago money. And the other way around—if the Parkers had given more than Dad, they could have kept Parker there. It was only a question of how much, not where it came from. But if the Parker kid had been connected to the Schreckers or some other New

Englanders, then Dad's money wouldn't have been as good. A Schrecker dollar was holy or something. No one up there thought it was just like a dollar anywhere else, just green paper with numbers on it.

The other big trouble was that Campbell *was* a little nuts. He admitted it himself. His admitting it made it seem less serious, but it was still there. Of course, he had plenty of reason to be nuts, after what he'd been through, but that only explained why—it didn't change it.

And he wasn't a fighter. I don't know if that was because he was a little nuts, or if he was a little nuts because he wasn't a fighter. When I told him that if I was in his place I'd cry and slobber and make a mess out of everything, he had said that they'd just call him nuttier. And maybe that was true for him, but it wouldn't have been true for me. I'm not really all that much of a fighter, but I fight for things I want. I guess I'm a little like Dad that way. I think Campbell's trouble with the Schreckers was that they were so nasty they made him sick, and sort of paralyzed him. But if you're a kid who's a fighter, you always try to make people sicker than they make you. There's no limit to what you do when you have to.

You roll around and moan and make such a mess that they get disgusted. They get sick of it and decide they don't want any more. It may be a mean way to fight, but if you're a kid you have to use all the weapons you have. Campbell just wasn't up to it, he just wasn't a fighter.

11

THE NEXT DAY we were all back at the old grind, and the day before was like a dream. On top of all the sports and listening to the Skipper, Lattimore and I were supposed to be thinking about how to help Campbell. It's hard to do that when you're bouncing along on a horse or playing tennis.

Campbell himself was pretty good. I mean, he didn't sit around and ask us if we'd thought of anything. He didn't say much at all, just did the sports and kept his mouth shut.

The three of us could have hung around together in our free time and talked about it, but we knew that would look funny, so we kept split up.

After dinner the next day we were all in the main

lodge. Lattimore was writing letters and Campbell had a book and I let Russell, the black kid from Groton, try to teach me chess.

"You could learn if you tried," he said. I wasn't doing too well.

"But then I'd know something more," I said. "My brain couldn't take it."

"Your brain is *meant* to work," he said. "That's what it's for."

"Not mine," I told him. "Mine gets overheated if I use it too much. I have to give it plenty of rest."

Swanson was listening, of course, and trying to keep from saying anything.

"Maybe you're right at that," Russell said. "I suppose thinking does cause a lot of unhappiness."

"Now you're catching on," I told him.

Swanson opened his mouth to say something and Russell started talking about some other idea of his. Whether animals are happier than we are, I think it was. He talked so fast that Swanson had to close his mouth again. It was a new game we were playing with Swanson.

It made him mad, as usual, and when he did have a chance after a while he started bragging to some of the others about how he smoked pot all the time at Hotchkiss. "I had some with me when I first came up here," he said, "but it's all gone and I can't get any more."

"What's so great about pot?" some other kid asked him.

"It relaxes you," Swanson said. "Makes everything seem better. It takes you out of the ordinary world."

Then they talked about who smoked it and who didn't, and finally some kid asked me if I did.

I said no, and Swanson jumped up and down. "I didn't think so!" he yelled. "Too chicken! Too square!"

There were a few laughs, and I said, "No, just too slow."

"What do you mean, slow?" they asked me.

"Compared to a real sendoff," I said. "Like horse."

"Horse is the rocket," Russell agreed with me. "The thinking kid's best friend."

"Do you mainline?" Adams asked me.

"It's the only way," I said.

"How often do you do it?" he asked.

"It depends on your mood," I told him. "Usually a couple of times a week."

"Even up here?"

"He's got a pusher who meets him in the woods," Russell said. "Anything for an old customer."

"They're lying!" Swanson squealed, with his pimples like stoplights. "Ox doesn't take horse. He doesn't even have the guts to smoke pot. How could he be on horse?"

"I graduated," I told him.

Nobody knew what to believe and Swanson was even sorer than usual.

That night in the cabin Campbell told us that Paulson had talked to him in the afternoon and asked him what we'd done in Dexter the day before. "I guess he's supposed to report everything to the Schreckers," he said.

"What did you tell him?"

"Nothing much. Just said we'd had a good time."

Lattimore and I looked at each other. I knew what he was thinking, that he or I wouldn't have even said that much. We would have said, "Oh, it was all right, if you like family afternoons," hinting that we didn't.

"Did he ask you a lot of questions?" Lattimore asked him.

"Naturally," Campbell said. "All about your mother and your sister and what was said. But don't worry, I didn't tell him anything. The only thing I said was that we had a good time and that we were all pretty good friends."

"Why did you tell him we were all good friends?" I asked Campbell. I was beginning to get a funny feeling in my stomach.

"I thought it would be good for the Schreckers to find out I have some friends," Campbell said. "Then they won't think I'm alone. They may even decide they have to watch their step."

"That's one way to look at it," Lattimore said. "But you don't want to tip your hand." He looked a little upset, too.

"I won't," Campbell said. "Don't forget I've been in this for a long time. I know how to be careful."

The words sounded all right, but he said them in a cocky way that made you wonder.

Lattimore and I didn't say any more that night—
and with Campbell there we couldn't have talked to
each other anyhow—but we were thinking the same
thing, I knew. Campbell hadn't had any friends for
so long that he couldn't help letting it go to his head.
I would have bet that when he talked to Paulson and
said we were all good friends he'd said it in the same
cocky, bragging way. And that wasn't good for any of
us.

The next day during riding Lattimore said, "I hope
he didn't blow it with Paulson."

"I hope so, too."

But he had. When we came back from tennis that
afternoon, Campbell was gone, and all his stuff with
him.

12

WE JUST STOOD THERE and looked at each other.

"Someone's grabbed him," Lattimore said. "But who? The Schreckers? Paulson? The psychiatrist from Boston?"

"We'll have to ask," I said.

"*Ask?*"

"Yes, ask. Our roommate disappears, and so the natural thing to do is ask where he went. It would look funny if we didn't."

"Yes, I guess you're right. But who do we ask?"

"Paulson, the Skipper . . ."

"They won't tell us the truth."

"They won't tell us why he was grabbed, but I bet they'll tell us where he's been taken."

"The moron!" Lattimore said. "He couldn't keep his mouth shut."

"I wonder if we could, in his shoes."

It turned out we didn't have to ask where he'd gone —even though we did to keep up appearances. Because there was a note stuck in the pocket of the jacket I always wore to dinner, and I found it when I changed.

"Paulson called Schreckers," it read. "They came and told the Skipper they were furious he had allowed me off the grounds. So they're taking me out of Downing for the rest of the summer. I'll be at Pilgrim's Knob under tight guard, I guess. Can you get me out? Thanks. Campbell."

"Don't tell me that's not a dumb note," Lattimore said.

He was right. Campbell had gotten himself grabbed, and now he expected us to spring him. He wanted other people to help him, but he was stupid and lazy about helping himself. He was what they call a parasite. It was part of his nervousness and nuttiness, so it wasn't all his fault the way it would have been if he was normal, but it was still a pain.

"It's dumb all right," I said.

"I know, I know," Lattimore said. "It's not all his fault that he's dumb. But we can't help him if he won't sober up."

"Maybe we can't even if he does," I said. "They've really got him now."

We talked about it and decided we'd have to ask

where he was so it would look normal. Then we'd try to figure something out.

I tackled the Skipper and Lattimore went to see Paulson.

I found the Skipper just outside the dining hall and asked him if he had a minute.

"Well, well," he said. "Ox—I mean Carter—you're growing. Fine, big boy, already as tall as I am—no, I think a bit taller. The outdoor life must be agreeing . . . "

"My last name is Olmstead," I said. "But that doesn't matter. I have to tell you that Campbell is gone from the cabin, and so is all his stuff. We can't figure out if he's run away or what. But I knew I should tell you he's gone."

He looked at me for a minute without saying anything, and I wondered if he wanted to call Campbell a runaway and let it go at that, because then he wouldn't have to explain anything. But if he did that, he'd have to pretend to call the cops. It was too complicated, though, so he finally sighed and gave that idea up and said, "His grandparents came and got him. It's your fault."

"*My* fault?"

"Yours and Lattimore's. And Mrs. Lattimore's. You took him away from camp yesterday."

"We had permission," I said. "You gave it yourself."

"Yes, I'm to blame, too," he said. "I forgot that the Schreckers had left an order—a request, I should say— that he not leave Camp Downing for any reason. But the real damage was that you had such a good time. *That* wasn't my fault."

He said the last part in a whine, just like a little kid, and I almost laughed.

"Why was it so bad to have a good time?" I asked him.

"It isn't good for Campbell to enjoy himself. That's what all the doctors tell the Schreckers. It gets him excited in a bad way and he goes completely to pieces later. That's why they came and got him, because they thought—with reason, I must admit—that Camp Downing had become . . . dangerous for him."

"Aw, Skipper, do you believe all that?"

He stared at me. "Are you suggesting that the Schreckers aren't completely honorable people?" he asked me in a nasty way.

"I'm only suggesting that it can't be all bad for someone to enjoy himself."

"Are you an expert?"

"I'm a human being."

"You're a boy."

"You mean the two are different?"

"You're talking very foolishly. And it's time for dinner."

So we went into the dining hall and he prayed and the rest of us listened.

After dinner everyone was asking Lattimore and me what had happened to Campbell. We only told them that his grandparents had picked him up and we didn't know why.

We got out of the hall and down to our cabin as soon as we could. Then I told Lattimore about the Skipper and he told me about Paulson. I told him about the Skipper first, and he was laughing at the end.

"I shouldn't laugh," he said, "but there's something about the stuff you can get into . . . "

"Tell me about Paulson."

"Tried to be very smooth. Said he was under a professional obligation to tell the Schreckers anything unusual about Campbell. Said Campbell seemed slightly hysterical when he was talking about his outing, so he had to call the Schreckers and tell them that. Said he himself didn't think it was all that serious, but they are very concerned people and know more about the 'case' than he does, so if they felt it was the wrong atmosphere here for Campbell, he'd have to go along with that. He tried a little smile on me and said he thought the Schreckers might be just a tiny bit jealous of Campbell's new pals. But the minute he said that he tried to take it back. I asked him if Campbell went quietly, and he said he did. But get this—then he said, 'I warned him that if he threw a scene I'd have to give him an injection.' So Campbell probably figured he'd better stay conscious so he could get the note to us. You can hardly blame him for not fighting them, not with that hypodermic waiting for him if he did."

"It's like something in the movies or on TV," I said. "It's like what the Russians do, dragging people around unconscious and putting them on planes." For the first time I was really sort of sick to my stomach at what was done to Campbell, and what he had been threatened with. And sick about the people who did it, all pretending to be so respectable.

"It's terrible," Lattimore said, and I knew he was feeling the same way.

"You know, we have to do something about it. And I don't mean just because of Campbell. We have to do it for ourselves. We can't sit here and do nothing."

"No, we can't," Lattimore said. "But what do we do? That's the problem."

"No, the problem is deciding that we're going to do something."

"All right, that's the problem. And we've decided it. Now what?"

"I don't know yet. Don't rush me."

"To do anything we have to get out of Camp Downing. How can we do that?"

"Walk out."

"They'll look for us."

"But that doesn't mean they'll find us."

"And then there's money."

"I've got some."

"Not enough."

"Oh, I don't know. Isn't a grand enough? I've got that much."

"You do not."

"Careful what you say to a kid from Palm Beach about money."

"I guess that's true, Ox. But a *grand*?"

I picked up a chair and carried it over under the stuffed bird and got on it and reached through the hole in the feathers and hauled out my wad.

"Count it," I said, and tossed it to him.

When he finished he put it down and said, "All right, Ox, I beg your pardon. And I can tell you it's about the first time I've ever had to do that with anyone. I won't doubt you again. I'm a believer."

"You don't need to make that much out of it."

"I'm not so sure. A kid who can come up with a grand at the right time—well, if that doesn't mean something, I don't know what does. Do you always pack that much?"

I was going to tell him about my grandmother, and then I decided not to spoil it for him.

"Sometimes I have two or three," I told him.

We had the money, and the next thing was how to leave. Lattimore figured that out.

"We might as well have some fun," he said. "We'll pack all our stuff and clear out tomorrow night."

"Then the Skipper will tell the cops."

"We'll leave a note from the Schreckers. It'll say, 'We like kids, so we've taken Lattimore and Olmstead, too.' The Skipper won't know what to do. By the time he gets everything straightened out, we'll be there."

"Where?"

"Taddington, of course."

"Where'll we stay?"

"We'll find a place."

"What kind of place?"

"Leave it to me."

"I guess you know that if we go to a hotel or anything like that, they'll . . . "

"Leave it to me," he said. "Have faith."

"All right," I said. "But just tell me one thing—how are we going to get there?"

"I've got that figured out, too. Taddington is only thirty miles. We'll ride, like Paul Revere."

"*Ride?*" I almost had a heart attack.

"It beats walking, and we can't get out on the highways and hitchhike. We'll go by back roads—I'll get a map—and it'll only take five or six hours."

"What'll we do with the horses when we get there?"

He threw up his hands. "How do I know? Sell 'em, keep 'em, give 'em to some farmer."

We talked over the details, and by the time we went to sleep we had our plans all made.

That night I had a sort of gruesome dream. Lattimore and I were breaking into Pilgrim's Knob to get Campbell, and the Schreckers caught us at it. They were yelling and cursing and throwing things at us. We dodged around and got out of the house, but they came after us. Dr. Schrecker's wheel chair had an engine on it, a big one, and Mrs. Schrecker rode on the back of the chair like the driver on one of those dog teams in the Far North. His face was wild, with the lips pulled back and the teeth hanging out, and hers was about the same. They were like a pair of married witches, and the wheel chair was so fast we couldn't get away from it. It was gaining on us and twisting and turning through the trees and the Schreckers were shrieking with joy and then we got behind a tree and the chair roared past and I started running because I knew it would be right back. "Don't run," Lattimore called after me. "They aren't coming back." "That's what you think," I said. "No sweat," he said, "I cut his brake cables." So I came back and we were waiting for the crash when the end of the dream came.

I think I dreamed it that way because Lattimore did think of everything. I wouldn't put it past him to have thought of the brake cables in real life.

The next day we did everything in the same old way. Calisthenics, breakfast, riding, swimming, lunch, rest, riding, and tennis. Every time we finished one more step, I told myself that was the last time for that, and by the time we got to dinner I was feeling very good.

Before dinner Lattimore went to the pay phone booth to call Anne to have her tell his mother not to worry if they heard he'd been kidnapped. He was going to tell her some of what was going on, and that we'd be in touch.

I was lying on my bed taking a little rest after he went, when Peabody came into the cabin.

"Skipper wants to see you," he said. "Right now."

"What for?"

"You'll find out."

I got up and followed him up to the Skipper's office, and I went in alone.

He didn't give me any kind of smile at all, the way he usually did, but started right in. "Ox—I mean Olmstead—something very serious has been brought to my attention. I have it from a reliable source that you are taking horse—I mean heroin—here at Camp Downing. That you have your own pusher—as it's called—who comes up here and meets you in the woods."

I thought he was going to ask me then if it was true or not, but he just kept going.

"Now, Ox, I think every boy who has ever been at Downing knows that the Skipper plays fair. I'm as tolerant as they come. But drugs, hard drugs, are too much. I know that all you boys take an occasional whiff of pot. I know that, we all know it. It may surprise you to find out that I've even taken a whiff myself with boys who have been honest enough to come to me and tell me frankly that they use pot. Boys, I hardly need add, who have shown me that they are dedicated. I learned a long time ago that if you can't lick 'em, you have to join 'em. I don't mean I'm whiffing all the time—and I don't want that impression to get started, to get headway—because these occasions are rare. They are limited to sessions with dedicated boys. Don't forget that it's been medically proved that pot is not nearly so bad for you as liquor. Or even ordinary tobacco. I'd a hundred times rather see a boy smoke an occasional joint than drink beer all summer. Or even smoke regular cigarettes. And I'm backed up by medical opinion."

He stopped as though he'd forgotten what he was

getting to, but then he remembered. *"However,* horse is a different kettle of fish," he said, and wagged his finger at me very slowly. "At Camp Downing, horse is out. *Absolutely out.* Am I clear?"

I started to say that I didn't have anything to do with horse, but by then he wasn't even looking at me. He had picked up his pencil and was working on a chart for the tennis tournament. "That's all," he said, with his head bent down over the chart. "And tell your pusher to stay out of these woods."

I was just about out the door when he said, "Think of the younger boys." You could tell from the tone of his voice that his mind was on something else. In camps they're always telling you to think of the younger boys. It's a reflex.

When I left the Skipper's office, I found Peabody trying to listen at the door, and after I closed it he said, "What was all that about?"

"He doesn't want horse pushers in the woods," I told him.

"He doesn't what?" Peabody asked me, but I kept going and left him to figure it out.

I told Lattimore about it before dinner and he said, "That's what's called 'the concerned camp director.'" Then he told me Anne thought it was great we were taking off, and would do her part in keeping things calm.

Right after dinner Swanson came up to me and asked what the Skipper had wanted.

"He said you told him I was on horse," I said. "We

had a good laugh about it. He said that now I have my growth it won't hurt me."

"I'll bet," Swanson said.

"How much?"

"More than you've got."

"I've got enough for you."

"I don't think you do," Swanson said. "I don't think you're as rich as you say you are. I think you're a phony."

"I'll bet he has more money in his pocket right now than you have," Lattimore said.

"Watch out," Cabot said. "He just got a check from his father today. It was a big one too, because he's supposed to buy his fare home out of it."

"Did he cash it?" Lattimore asked.

"I cashed it," Swanson said, "and I've got it all right here." He patted his pants pocket.

"Gee, I don't know, Lattimore," I said. "He's loaded."

"I thought you'd back down," Swanson said.

"Tell you what," Lattimore said to him. "You and Ox empty out. Whoever has the most takes the other one's pile. Winner takes all."

Swanson hesitated a minute and stared at me. I looked as worried as I could. Then he made up his mind and said, "OK, but don't say you weren't warned." He pulled out a roll and spread it on a table. "Two hundred and fifty," he said, and looked around like he'd laid down a million.

I kept the worried look and pulled out my roll, that

I'd been carrying since I took it out of the bird. Then I peeled off three hundreds and laid them down.

"That's right," Lattimore said. "Just enough to top him. No point in being a show-off."

"Satisfied?" I said to Swanson. He had a sick look on his face and seemed kind of frozen. Even his pimples had lost all their color. Then he finally nodded and I picked up both piles.

"How much *do* you have in that roll of yours?" Cabot asked me.

"He was only packing a couple of grand tonight," Lattimore said. "One of his oil wells is having repairs."

"You don't have two grand there!" Cabot said.

"Want to bet?" Lattimore asked, and Cabot didn't.

Swanson looked punchy, but I decided to give him the last push. After all, he had tried to get me kicked out of camp.

"When the Skipper and I finished laughing about your telling him I was on horse, we got serious," I said. "I told him you were the pusher here."

"He wouldn't believe that," Swanson said.

"Wait until tomorrow," I said. "He's phoning your parents now."

Swanson really looked sick then. Mean kids always have mean parents, and I knew his were probably terrible to him. When he had to explain to them about losing the two-fifty they'd tear him to pieces. Then pushing horse on top of that. He had reason to worry. I almost handed him back the two-fifty and told him no one was phoning his parents about pushing, but something stopped me. He had to learn sometime not to keep acting like such a pain. And to stop kidding himself about his parents and his situation. If I'd handed the money back he just would have thought he was perfect all over again. I don't mean I kept it for his sake or anything like that. I only mean that I felt sorry for him for a second, and then I remembered plenty of reasons not to be.

When we got back to the cabin, I said to Lattimore, "Was that so smart? Now they'll know we started with a big roll."

"I thought it was better they know that," Lattimore said. "Then they won't worry about us. And besides, I felt sort of shy about your putting up all the money."

"Are you suggesting you won that two-fifty? I thought I did."

"I talked him into the bet," Lattimore said.

"All right," I said. "Here it is." And I tossed him the two-fifty.

"I was kidding," he said. "It's yours."

"Keep it," I told him. "Call it walking-around money."

"Those Palm Beach expressions," Lattimore said, shaking his head like he was filled with admiration.

"That's not a Palm Beach expression," I said. "Not originally, anyhow. It's from Las Vegas, or somewhere."

Then we packed up, which didn't take long, and left the note from the Schreckers, printed out in block letters. Lattimore had added a little, so now it read: "We like kids, so we've taken Lattimore and Olmstead, too. They need help. We'll call you when they're on their feet." It was signed "The Schreckers."

"I think the Skipper will really believe it," Lattimore said. "It's got that authentic Schrecker ring."

We crept down to the stables carrying our suitcases.

"Which horse do you want?" Lattimore asked me.

"I'd better stick to Klondike," I said. "I wouldn't like to try my riding style on any of the others."

"But if you take Klondike, they'll know . . . but I've got the answer to that." He laughed.

"Let me in on it."

"We'll take the whole bunch, all eighty of them, John Wayne style. Then they won't know who took what horse."

I thought it was going to be a lot of trouble, but you couldn't change his mind when he got an idea like that.

It turned out to be easy, though, because at night the horses were outside in a pasture near the stables. All we had to do was saddle up our own and put the suitcases on another one—the "pack horse," Lattimore called him—and then open the pasture gate and start riding. All the others trooped after us. Before we left, Lattimore took a piece of chalk and wrote on the fence, "Needed some extra horses tonight. Thanks. The Connollys."

We walked them slowly until we were about a mile from the camp. We came into a big meadow there, and just for fun we galloped through it, with the whole bunch pounding along behind. We were almost to the woods on the other side when we suddenly noticed a gang of people ahead of us, running for their lives to stay out of the way of the horses. We swerved to one side, and most of the horses swerved with us, but some didn't. As we went by we could see a big tangle of horses and people.

"The Connollys," Lattimore yelled at me when we we were past. "Out for a stroll. Finally got some of their own back."

13

WE RODE ALL NIGHT. It nearly killed me, especially with the way I had to ride, and old Klondike shaking worse every mile. But I stuck on.

One of our biggest problems was getting rid of the other horses. Quite a few had stayed behind with the Connollys, but we still had about fifty trailing after us. We were on back roads by then, and we were afraid some car would come along and the driver would start wondering what fifty horses and a couple of riders were doing out at midnight.

Finally we got to the edge of a farm that was fenced. We found a gate without a lock and opened it and rode in and the whole troop came with us. Then we rode our own horses back out and shut the gate before the rest could follow.

"There'll be a surprised farmer tomorrow morning," Lattimore said.

"We aren't exactly making a quiet exit from Camp Downing," I said.

"We're making a perfect exit," he said. "We've created so many diversions they won't know where we've gone. Running into the Connollys was a great stroke of luck. Now the Skipper will have to think they did take the horses, just as the note on the fence said."

"I hope there are some Connollys left for him to blame. Those horses really ran into them."

"They're tough," Lattimore said. "But can't you just see the Skipper when someone comes in and tells him about horses and Connollys in the woods? He'll get it all mixed up with pushing horse in the woods. I wouldn't be surprised if he ends up thinking the Connollys are all using horse."

"Or are all pushers."

"That's better. Anyhow, the great thing is diversion. Get 'em off the track. That's why I sent the postcards."

"What postcards?"

"To the Schreckers. I sent about ten yesterday. All kinds. 'If you don't let Campbell go, I'm calling the New England Medical Association. Dr. Paulson.' And 'I'm coming after you. The Skipper.' Those were to get them off balance. Then some silly ones to make them mad. Like, 'Where was Dr. Schrecker when the lights went out? Down in the dungeons eating sourkraut?' I spelled it s-o-u-r because that's the way he is. And his name being German, too. No signature on that one. The cards are a way of telling Campbell we're active, as well as keeping the Schreckers off base."

"You're busy when you get going," I told him, and I meant it. I never saw a kid who could think of as much stuff as Lattimore.

We rode along and he talked. I didn't say much because just staying on Klondike was enough to keep me busy. But I didn't mind Lattimore talking because it helped a little to keep my mind off the riding.

"You're pretty quiet," he finally said.

"I've got problems," I said.

"Let's talk Schrecker talk," he said. "That'll cheer you up. I'll be the mad doctor and you be Mrs. S."

"I can't do that stuff," I told him.

"OK," he said. "I'll be Mrs. S. and you be the mad doctor. I'll start. It's breakfast time at Pilgrim's Knob, and she pours him a cup of coffee and then she says, 'Grampy, I'm so concerned this morning about Betty. She and Phil just don't seem to be able to see their own best interests about the land that Betty's father left to them.' "

He stopped. I didn't say anything, and then he said, "Now it's your turn."

"To do what?"

"To say something. You're the mad doctor, say something."

"What'll I say?"

"The first thing that comes into your head, if you were the mad doctor."

"Who's Betty?"

"Why, Grampy, don't you remember Betty and Phil? Betty is your cousin George's sister-in-law's niece. And Phil is her husband. They're lovely people, but they make mistakes. They've inherited this land next to that big piece we own out in New Mexico and now they won't sell it to us at our price. That's why we're so concerned about them. We think they're nuts. Asking for the booby hatch."

He stopped again.

"I can't do it," I told him. "I can't act the way you can."

"All right," he said. "I'll play both parts. What Grampy says to that is something like this . . . 'I hate to see nice young people going nuts like that, but if they do, if they won't play the game, then I say there's always room for one more in the booby hatch.' And then she says . . ."

He went on like that for hours. He could even imitate their voices. The mad doctor with sort of a growl, and Mrs. Schrecker with all that breath. Her voice was deep, too, and he got that down just right. It was like listening to a soap opera on TV. By the time we got to the outskirts of Taddington, they'd put about thirty people in the booby hatch and collected about five million in trust funds and land and houses and stocks and everything else you could think of. They even mopped up fur coats and jewelry. "Anything of value," was the expression he had them using all the time. "If there's anything of value, it will help to pay the bills at the booby hatch, so you'd better turn it over to us."

140

In really bad cases they'd use rough stuff, or get one of their lawyers or judges to.

It was sort of fun to listen to and, as I said, it made the ride easier.

The dawn was just breaking when we stopped. We were about a couple of miles from Taddington, and a little above it on a dirt road. Taddington was bigger than I thought and it looked pretty.

Even Lattimore was dead tired by that time, and I was gone. I was trying to figure out the next move when a voice behind me said, "Good morning."

We turned around and it was an old man, out for a walk, I guess. There are people like that who get up before dawn and walk around. He had on rough clothes and was about sixty, but in good shape. He was staring at us hard and I realized how bad we looked. Dressed in dirty riding clothes, fagged out, me with my rear end in the air, the pack horse with the suitcases tied on, and Klondike shaking all over. We knew we were a sight and he was taking it all in.

We said good morning to him and he said, "You look pretty tired."

"We are," Lattimore said. "We've been riding most of the night. It's a survival test organized by our camp. Camp Sheldon."

That was the story we had made up in case we ran into anyone. There was a real Camp Sheldon, only it was in the opposite direction from Camp Downing.

"An all-night ride?" the man asked us. "Isn't that quite a lot?"

"We're very active at Sheldon," Lattimore said.

141

"Now we have to ride back there. All part of the contest."

"How far is it?"

"About twenty miles."

"But where will you have breakfast?"

"We have some stuff with us. Well, Mister, I guess we better be off. We're looking for the contest route now. It's supposed to be marked, but you know how these instructors are. Too lazy to do it right. I do know it's supposed to go by a place that belongs to a lady named Tompkins and then . . . "

"Oh, you're a ways off," he said. "That's a mile or two from here. The old Tompkins quarry."

"Could you tell us how to get there?"

So he did. It was complicated, down one road and up another and a left and two rights and so on. I couldn't remember it, but I knew Lattimore would so I didn't try.

Then we said good-bye to him and started off again.

"What's this Tompkins business?" I asked Lattimore.

"Do you remember Campbell saying there were a few people in Taddington who didn't like the Schreckers? One woman in particular, but he didn't remember the name?"

"I remember something about it."

"I asked Anne to find that name if she could, through the girl she knows who visits here. Last night when I called her, she gave me the lady's name— Tompkins. Anne isn't sure it's the right woman, but she thinks it probably is."

"What if it isn't?"

"We have to take the chance. We can't just float around here."

We got to the Tompkins place about half an hour later. We knew it from the way the man had described it. It was a grim-looking spot, with half a mountain torn off where they'd had the quarry, and all the bare rock and pits and sheds and rusted machinery still there. There was a rough dirt road from the quarry back to the house. You went through the part where they had a farm once, but now it was all gone to pieces, with the fences falling apart and the trees looking dead. The house was what they call the Victorian style, with all that fancy woodwork carving outside and lightning rods everywhere. The paint had all worn off, but you could see it had been quite a place in its day.

We were riding up toward it and we were almost at the front steps when this woman came out on the porch and stood there. She had long, yellowish-white hair and wild eyes, and she was moving all over the place one minute and the next she was standing so still you could hardly believe it.

We stopped and waited and she stood there without saying anything. She was wearing an old dress and broken-down shoes, but she looked like someone important. Her arms were folded, and finally she said, "You are on my land. I advise you to get off it."

She had a strong voice and it was wonderful the way it carried. She spoke in an ordinary way, but it carried fifty feet, like she was standing next to you.

"We're lost," Lattimore said.

"No one gets lost here," she said. The morning light was on her face and she looked sort of noble under everything.

"We've been riding all night," Lattimore said.

"I've been thinking all night," she said. "But I'm not trespassing this morning."

"Well, we're not lost," Lattimore said. "We came here to see you."

"What about?"

"If you'll let us get down off these horses, I'll tell you."

I didn't think she would, but she did. She looked at both of us carefully, and then she said, "You can put your horses in the barn. There's some hay in there. I'll be waiting inside." And she turned and walked back into the house. She walked straight and with a lot of pride.

"This isn't bad," Lattimore said when we got in the barn. "At least the horses are out of sight."

"But that woman, she . . . "

"Let's settle the horses first."

I was so thankful to be off Klondike that I didn't argue.

"Do you know how to feed 'em?" I asked him.

"Throw out some hay."

"Is that all? What about rubdowns and the rest?" The stable hands did it at Downing—I didn't have any idea of how you were supposed to take care of a horse.

"These are tough horses," Lattimore said. "They don't need all that babying."

So we just pulled off the saddles and bridles and threw out some hay and let them eat and dry off on their own.

Then I put it to Lattimore. "What if this woman turns out to be a friend of the Schreckers after all? She seems plenty strange."

"I don't think she will," he said. "She's strange, but she doesn't look like a phony. Or act like one. Otherwise, I wouldn't have stayed."

"No, she doesn't seem phony. But you never know."

"We'll be careful," Lattimore said.

We went back to the house and knocked on the front door. There was no answer so we went in. The rooms were big and filled with old furniture and covered with dust and cobwebs. We wandered around for a while and then found her in the dining room. She was sitting at a big round table. There was a coffeepot and three cups on the table, nothing else.

"Sit down," she said, acting like some ancient princess.

We sat and she poured out the coffee. When she handed me my cup she looked at me and smiled in a way. It was a peculiar smile, because some of her teeth were discolored and chipped.

"You look as though you were expecting more than coffee," she said.

"I'm sorry," I said, "but I'm big and I'm still growing."

"Maybe you'll get something more substantial later," she said. Then her eyes whirled around for a minute. It was hard for her to stay on the track. We were going to find that out. "I am Dacoolah Tompkins," she said, drawing herself up. "I am the last of the Taddington Tompkinses. I was a great actress, although you are too young to realize that. I was a figure on the stage. Now I try to remember, to remember and write the story of my life in some sort of style . . . in some sort of sequence . . . in some way . . . "

Her voice trailed off and we waited for more. You could tell she'd been a good actress from the way she talked and because you wanted to hear her go on.

"Now, what are you doing here?" she asked Lattimore. She went back and forth like that, from her problems to yours.

"We have to start somewhere," Lattimore said to me. "How about it?"

He was asking me if I trusted her, and even though I could see she was a little off, I thought she was as good a bet as anyone else we were likely to run into, so I said, "OK."

"Do you know some people named Schrecker here in Taddington, Mrs. Tompkins?" Lattimore asked her.

"I am not *Mrs.* Tompkins," she blazed at him. "I am not *Miss* Tompkins. I am *Dacoolah* Tompkins. You will call me Dacoolah. Do you understand that?"

"Yes," he said.

"Yes what?"

"Yes, Dacoolah."

She looked at me, and I had to say "Yes, Dacoolah" too.

146

"It's a pretty name," Lattimore said.

"It's a silly name," she said in a bored way, looking into her coffee cup, "but it served its purpose. Famous once, up in lights, but you're too young to have seen that.

"Why did my parents call me Dacoolah? They didn't. I was christened Hortense, fine for New England but unsuitable for the stage. Unthinkable. My first husband to the rescue. He was traveling in the South and called one night to say he was in jail. At least that's what I thought he said, in his Southern accent. 'I am in da coolah' was what I understood, but he was saying that he was in a place called Dacoolah, Georgia, and not in the pokey at all.

"We later had what used to be called a hearty laugh about the whole thing, and on the strength of that laugh and a great deal of gin I gave up Hortense for Dacoolah. It changed my life in many ways . . . everyone thought I was from the South in a few years, and I half believed it myself. Southern actresses were supposed to be more sensitive, deeper, more morbid . . . I suppose I still believe it. Ghostly plantations, Truman Capote and Tennessee Williams hanging from the biggest magnolia tree. . . . My first husband, poor Randolph . . . I don't know the Schreckers intimately, but I know them."

I thought she'd forgotten Lattimore asking her about the Schreckers, and that she was going to wander on all night about herself, but she sort of snapped back suddenly. She did that.

"What do you think of them?" Lattimore asked her.

"I think they're terrible," she said.

"From what we hear, you must be the only person in town who does," I said.

"Perhaps," she said. "But I can afford to stand alone. They're impossible, insufferable, preposterous people. If everyone else thinks they're wonderful . . . well, that's what makes what we quaintly used to call 'show business.' "

"We don't think they're wonderful," Lattimore said. "We think they're the way you say they are. Only worse, because we know more about them."

"You do?" Dacoolah was really interested at that, interested for the first time.

"I'm going to tell you the truth, Dacoolah," Lattimore said. "And I only want to ask you one thing first. Not to repeat any of it later. Or to tell anyone we're here."

"I have no friends," she said. "Not any more. I couldn't betray anyone if I wanted." She said that with just the right touch. It was real acting.

"We're from Camp Downing," Lattimore said. "Tommy Campbell, the kid who lives with the Schreckers, was our cabin mate there. He told us how they're working on him to get his money. Then the day before yesterday, they grabbed him out of Downing and took him home. We're here to help him, to get him out of that house if we can."

"Why did you come to me?"

Lattimore explained how Campbell had told us

148

there was someone in Taddington who didn't like the Schreckers, and how Anne had found out her name. He didn't say that Campbell had called her a crazy old actress. He just said actress.

"I have heard of the boy's troubles," she said. "But in the upside-down Taddington version, of course. Just another trial for the sainted Schreckers. . . . What if you do get him out of the house? What then? Where will he go?"

"We haven't thought that far yet," Lattimore said. "If we can get him out, maybe we can get some influential people interested in the case, and maybe they'll make enough noise so he won't have to go back."

"And you want a place to stay to stay while you do all this," Dacoolah said.

"We were hoping for one," Lattimore said. "We have plenty of money. We could pay."

"And I could use the money," she muttered. She leaned back and got ready to play another scene. "Suppose a couple of boys came along and moved into my barn for a few days. I wouldn't necessarily even know they were there, would I? If they got into some scrape and what passes for the authorities came to me, I could always say I didn't know what was going on. Right?"

"You're a pal," I said.

"Those boys will have to come and go by the back path," she said, talking like she hadn't heard me. "They'll also have to get rid of their horses. And they'll have to promise me that no matter what hap-

149

pens they won't tell anyone about talking to me. They never met me, they just slipped into the barn on their own. That sounds cowardly on my part, but the fact is that no matter what the boys do they won't get into any trouble, because they're boys. Dacoolah is supposed to be an adult and know better, so Dacoolah could get in trouble—plenty of trouble—if anyone thought Dacoolah had aided and abetted them."

"We understand," Lattimore said.

"You're a real pal," I said. "I mean, Dacoolah is a real pal."

"Those boys say they can pay," she said. "Can they pay . . . a hundred?"

"They can," Lattimore said. She had us talking that way by then. "Put it on the table, Ox."

I dug out the roll and peeled off a hundred and laid it down. Her eyes really lit up.

"You do have it!" she cried out. "You're *real!*" Then she pushed it back. "No, I couldn't take it."

"Yes, you can," I said. At first I thought it wouldn't work to pay for help in a fight for right and wrong, but then I realized she was really poor and needed the money anyhow. In a separate way, just to stay alive.

"No," she said.

"He's rich," Lattimore said. "Like an angel in the theater."

"Oh," she said, "then it's all right, I'm sure." And she picked the hundred up and slid it into the front of that old dress. "But I'd have helped you anyhow, I hope you know that . . . maybe I should have asked for more, if you really are an angel. But if you aren't an angel in one way, you are in another, so . . . where was I? Yes, I'm still a person, still ready to work against nonpeople, the Schrecker types. But we're outnumbered, to say the least. However, you'll never regret having made a contribution to my war chest. Dacoolah delivers. A warm barn, plenty of hay to make beds with—one never sleeps better than on hay—and . . . well, moral support."

"We'll haul our own food in from now on, of course," Lattimore said, "but do you think we could have some breakfast? We're both hungry, but in Ox's case it's critical."

"You can have anything in the kitchen," Dacoolah said, "but I fear there isn't a great deal." She looked uncomfortable. "The larder is low."

"Let's look at it," I said. I was so starved I was ready to fall over.

We went out into the kitchen, and it was a sight. We learned later that she worked there on her book about her life because it was warmer in winter and cooler in summer. There were papers all over everything. And then dirty dishes and bottles and junk all over the papers.

"The typical artistic mess," she said, not a bit uncomfortable by then. She opened the door on the old refrigerator and there wasn't much there and what there was wasn't what anyone but her would be looking for. A lot of cold oatmeal and stale bread, a couple of dozen moldy hot dogs, and about a bucket of cole slaw. Then bags of prunes and raisins and stuff like that, with the sides pulled open. And six jars of mustard—I counted them. I didn't see any eggs or bacon or milk or orange juice or anything else I wanted. But I had to eat something, so I pulled out the hot dogs and the cole slaw. Lattimore took some prunes and raisins.

Dacoolah pushed some papers around on the big kitchen table and I sat down at an empty space and started in.

"Don't you want to cook those hot dogs—just warm them up?" Lattimore asked me.

"Too much work," I told him. Even good food isn't worth a lot of preparing, and the only thing to do with bad food is get it down quick and forget it, if you can.

It didn't take me long to knock those hot dogs off and when I finished I looked up and Lattimore and Dacoolah were both staring at me.

"Methinks there's an appetite there," she said, shaking her head. "Methinks" is Old English for "I think."

"I'm still growing," I said.

"If you could have seen yourself," Lattimore said. "How about some of the oatmeal?"

"No, thanks," I said. The hot dogs had tasted about a month old and the cole slaw not far behind—it had fizzed like it was fermenting into some kind of home-made drink. The whole mess felt like it might turn into some kind of dangerous chemical in my stomach, and I wasn't going to pile in any last-year's oatmeal on top of it and give it the final ingredient and have it go off. I was still hungry, but for once I had the sense to hold back.

Then Dacoolah asked us our names and we told her, and she asked us how long we thought what she called "Operation Schrecker" was going to take.

"Not more than a couple of days," Lattimore said.

"Won't they be tracking you from Camp Downing?"

"We left a lot of false trails."

"What about your parents?"

"Mine won't worry—my sister will take care of that. Ox's are too eccentric to worry."

"I'm from Palm Beach," I explained to Dacoolah. "The parents are different down there."

"They certainly have different children. And appropriately named. Ox was a brilliant choice in your case."

"It's my nickname. It's because I'm so big and mushy. Pretty obvious."

"How well you put it."

I think she was a little sore because I'd eaten all the hot dogs and cole slaw. But after a while she brightened up and told us some pretty good stories about being on the road in a play called *Hamlet*, by Shakespeare. She was Ophelia in the play, a character who goes out of her mind because Hamlet won't make his up. The actor who was playing Hamlet had a nervous breakdown on the stage one night and accused her of stealing his paycheck. You could see how that would have confused the audience—she did a wonderful job of

153

describing it, taking her part and his and then the parts of the manager and the other actors looking on from the sides, and even playing some people in the audience who thought it was all part of the play.

Then we were too tired to hear any more and went out to the barn and flattened out some hay in the loft and went to sleep. Hay doesn't look like much to sleep on, but it's not bad. Of course, being exhausted helps, too. It helped in another way, because if I hadn't been so worn out, the fight between the different kinds of stuff I'd eaten would have kept me awake in agony, so sometimes there's a lot to be said for being down and out.

We woke up at about three in the afternoon. My stomach was recovered and I was hungry for real food. Lattimore changed his clothes and went down to the town to buy some. I took Klondike and the other two horses out by the back path and walked for a mile or so along a trail on the edge of a stream. When we got to an open place I slipped off their bridles and left them there. The saddles were back in the barn, so they didn't have anything on.

They started munching grass before I was out of sight, and didn't try to follow me. Of course, I didn't like them much and they didn't like me, so there was no reason why they should tag after me.

I went back to the barn and lay around until Lattimore showed up with the food. He had plenty of bread and cheese and smoked ham and pickles and milk and crackers, and stuff to dip the crackers in, and canned olives and hard-boiled eggs and a dozen hamburgers and a roasted chicken and six quarts of root beer.

"This ought to hold you till tomorrow," he said. "If I'd been shopping for myself and one other normal appetite I would have bought about a quarter of what's here."

"No complaints," I said. "They don't suit you."

"Did you get rid of the horses?"

"Uh-huh."

While we ate we talked about Dacoolah and agreed that she was sort of a nut, but not bad. I told Lattimore I thought it was better to be nuts like that, and be able to tell stories and talk in a way that was interesting to other people, than to be nuts and just look out the window, and he said that was the way he felt, too.

Then we took another nap and when we woke up we got ready to go. We put on the best-looking clothes we had with us and brushed ourselves off and when it was just getting dark—around eight—we started off for Pilgrim's Knob.

14

IT WASN'T SO FAR AWAY, not more than a couple of miles. We stopped at a service station when we got down to the main road from the quarry, and the attendant told us where Pilgrim's Knob was. He was wagging his tail all over the place about the Schreckers, and when we walked away Lattimore said, "They probably buy their gas there."

"Or maybe they don't," I said. "And he wonders what's wrong with him."

"That's a fresh remark if I ever heard one," Lattimore said. "You must be feeling good."

"I don't feel so bad."

"I sent some postcards to the Schreckers today," he said. "A long one from the New England Medical As-

156

sociation saying they are sending a team down to investigate Dr. Paulson's complaint. Another one from Interpol saying they're alerted and on the case. And a few personal ones to the mad doctor from other lunatics."

"You mailed those in the Taddington post office?"

"Affirmative."

"You *are* a trouble-making kid."

"Hi'm sure tryin' to be. Hi'm doin' me bloomin' best, Sir." And he talked Cockney for a while.

We were walking along a country road with pretty expensive-looking houses set back from it. Each one had plenty of land, and trees that had been planted, and paddocks with horses in them. It wasn't really rich, but it wasn't poor, either.

"We're getting warm," I said, and Lattimore stopped the Cockney.

In another five minutes we were at the gate of Pilgrim's Knob.

The house itself sat up on a little hill. That's where the Knob part of the name came from. The Pilgrim part was because the Schreckers thought of themselves like that. It was because they were wild about religion. There was even a Pilgrim made out of iron on top of the gate. He had his arm stretched out to the house like he was pointing to some city in heaven.

It was dark by then, and we could see that the house was all lit up. It was about a quarter of a mile away, up on the hill.

"We can't just barge up the driveway," I said.

"We can start up that way," Lattimore said. "Then we'll branch off and circle through the trees and come to the back of the house."

That's what we did, and it didn't take long before we were in the bushes near the rear.

"I wish we knew which room is Campbell's," Lattimore said. "Then we could throw up a handful of pebbles and get him out here. I don't like the idea of going in there."

"You're telling me now?" I asked him. "I thought you had it all figured out."

"Let's take a turn around the house," he said.

So we slipped all the way around, staying near the trees. When we got to the front we could see that the driveway was full of cars.

"Party or council of war?" Lattimore said. "We have to get close enough to see."

We dodged from one car to another, and got up close to one of the side windows looking into the living room. It was full of people, all standing around Dr. Schrecker in his wheel chair. He was passing out postcards and they were reading them. While they read he was talking, and you could see that he was really sore. And the sorer he got, the sorer they got. They were all waving their postcards at each other and yelling around.

"My efforts are more appreciated than I'd hoped," Lattimore whispered.

It was kind of impressive, and my respect for Lattimore went up. Mrs. Schrecker was on the telephone, with a drink in her hand, and you could tell she was wild, too. Her lips were pulled back over her teeth, the way I had dreamed about her when she was riding on the back of the wheel chair.

"She's probably filling the President in," Lattimore said. "I wouldn't be surprised if they had a direct line."

Then a really strange thing happened. Some woman started laughing at one of the postcards, and Dr. Schrecker blew up. He waved his arms at her, and then he grabbed her by the wrist. He must have been twisting it, because she looked like it hurt. She tried to pull away, and a man who was probably her husband came over. I thought he was going to help her, but he started lecturing her. She was really hurting, but he didn't care, he was telling her where she was wrong. We could tell Dr. Schrecker wasn't going to let go until she gave in. Well, she finally did. We could see she was apologizing. Then Dr. Schrecker let her go, and she was rubbing her wrist and her husband took her off to finish his lecture. And all the time Dr. Schrecker had her by the wrist, Mrs. Schrecker was yelling from the telephone. She'd say a few words into the phone and then she'd yell a few at the woman, and so on. If she *had* had the President on the line, he would have had an earful.

"What a scene," Lattimore said. "Too bad Dacoolah can't see it. Well, I think we can try the rear. They all look pretty busy."

So we went back there, but on the other side from

159

the way we'd come. About halfway there, I saw some kind of building set in the trees and asked Lattimore what he thought it was.

"I don't know," he said. "Let's have a quick look."

We ducked down there and even before we'd gotten to it I could see that it looked like a tiny church, and Lattimore said, "It's a chapel. I should have known."

"What do you suppose they use it for?"

"They pray in it, you pagan. They hold services in it."

"How do you know?"

"It's not there to practice roller skating in. And besides, people like the Schreckers are always religious. Come on, we're wasting time."

We went up the path to the house and got around to the back. Lattimore opened the door and there was no one in the little hall. We went in and closed the door and went down the hall past the kitchen and a couple of utility rooms. There were back stairs and Lattimore started right up and I followed him. We could hear the voices from the front of the house, but they were pretty dim.

When we got to the second-floor landing there were about six or seven doors off the hall and then more stairs up to the third floor.

"He's probably on the third floor," Lattimore said, "but we'll check here first."

We opened all those doors and peeked in, and Campbell wasn't there. They were bedrooms and sitting rooms with that kind of wallpaper they use in

New England, and full of antique Colonial furniture. The house wasn't bad, but it certainly didn't look like real money, and I was wondering what they did with all the funds they were gobbling up.

Then we went up the stairs to the top floor and there were only three doors. We opened the one into Campbell's bedroom the first try.

He was lying on his bed reading a book and he almost jumped out of his skin when he saw us.

The first thing he said was, "How'd you get by the dogs?"

"We didn't see any dogs," I said.

"They must have them locked in the basement," he said. "They do that sometimes when they have a lot of people coming."

"Let's go," Lattimore said. "We're breaking you out."

We thought he'd jump at that, but he didn't do anything.

"Well, come on," Lattimore said. "We don't have all night."

"Come on where?" Campbell asked.

"We haven't figured that out yet, but we'll think of something," Lattimore said. He was so wrapped up in the problem that he wasn't noticing how Campbell was trying to get out of going.

"They'll just catch me and haul me back," Campbell said. "I told you that."

"Look, after you're out we're going to publicize what they've done. We'll get some people to help us.

You'll never have to come back here."

"You don't know the Schreckers," Campbell said. "You can't beat them."

Lattimore and I looked at each other. He finally got the message. It was the same old trouble with Campbell. Part nuts and completely scared.

"If you didn't want us to come and get you out, why did you ask us to in that note?" I said to him.

"I did then," he said, "but now I see it's hopeless."

Lattimore was really sore. "We rode all night," he said. "We got ourselves into big trouble everywhere. And all of it just to get you out. And now you fall apart on us. You're not worth helping. Come on, Ox, let's not waste any more breath on him. We'll leave him to the Schreckers. That's what he wants and that's what he deserves."

"I don't want to be the way I am," Campbell said, and he started to cry. "I want to get away from them. But I can't stand what they do when they get sore at me, and if I go and get caught again they'll be so sore that . . . I can only go if it's *sure*."

"What do you mean, *sure*?" Lattimore asked him. "If a battalion of Marines and the Air Force show up?"

"If it's fixed so I'm away from them legally," Campbell said.

"What do they do to you when they get sore?"

"They keep me up for hours talking. They don't beat me, but that talk is worse. They *believe* what they say, don't you see? They're so crazy that after five or six hours of it they can break you down. At least they can break me down. They've done it so often I can't stand it any more. If I escape now and have to come back, one more time would kill me. I'd be nuts forever. I know it."

He was crying and choking and could hardly talk. It was awful, but it made sense in a way. With Campbell, you always had to remember to look at it from his view, which was so different from Lattimore's or mine or any other kid's. Campbell had been pushed too far.

"All right, Campbell," Lattimore said, patting him on the arm, "you don't have to go with us now, but we'll still keep working to try to get you out the way you want. The legal way. How's that?"

Campbell stopped most of his choking and said, "That's my only chance. I wish I had enough guts to do it the other way, but I'm too shot. I'm sorry I'm such a mess, but I can't help it."

"We've got to go," Lattimore said. "But don't give up completely. We'll get you out yet. And in the meantime, don't tell anyone we were here."

"I won't," Campbell said.

"All right," Lattimore said. "So long for now."

We were almost out the door when Campbell said, "Those postcards are driving them wild. They know they're not from the people they're supposed to be from, but the idea of anyone making fun of them is too much."

"That's the general idea," Lattimore said. "Who do they think is sending them?"

"They aren't sure. One minute they think it's a kid, and then they say they're too sophisticated. No one has ever made such fun of them—no one's ever made any fun of them, come to think of it."

"Live and learn," Lattimore said.

Then we ducked out and down the stairs and out the back door again. I was listening for the dogs Campbell had talked about, and I thought I heard some snuffling near a door in the kitchen hall that could have been the door to the basement. I hoped they didn't get loose before we were out of Pilgrim's Knob, because if there's one thing I can't stand it's a dog after me.

But it was all right. We got out and back to the road without any trouble. When we worked past the living room, they were still all there, everyone with a postcard in his hand and the Schreckers laying down the law. The woman who'd been straightened out was sitting at the mad doctor's feet looking up at him in the wheel chair like he was the all-time holy man.

"Who do you suppose all those people are?" I asked Lattimore. There were over twenty of them, men and women and all well-dressed and sober.

"Friends, lawyers, solid citizens—every one of them ready to turn an insult to the Schreckers into an insult to themselves," he said.

"And the women?"

"Mostly wives, I guess. Haven't you ever seen wives before?"

"Sure, but these look so serious."

"What do they look like in Palm Beach?"

"They don't like to be serious there. They think they look older that way."

164

"Up here it's different."

Walking back I asked him why the Schreckers never beat Campbell up if they were so ready to pound other people around, like the wife who got of line.

"They're pros," he said. "They never do more than they have to. They can control Campbell with talk, so they skip the rough stuff. But with that woman . . . well, they didn't have time to talk to her for six hours. It had to be fast. Besides, remember that with Campbell they're playing for big stakes and he's got to be put away just right. They can't spend that much time on every woman who strolls in."

We walked along in silence for a while, and then Lattimore said, "Well, I guess that's the end of that. I don't see how we can get the adults to help spring him legally. If he'd only come with us, we could. But without him with us, we don't have any way of proving to people what's going on there."

"I guess you're right."

"I don't blame him. He's too pathetic to blame. But I just don't see how we can pull it off."

Lattimore sounded more discouraged that I'd ever heard him, but there was plenty to be discouraged about.

"Maybe something will turn up," I said, but I was only saying it to say something. I suppose Lattimore knew that, because he didn't answer. We walked all the way back to the quarry without talking.

15

THERE WAS A LIGHT on in the barn when we came down the rear path, and Dacoolah was sitting in there waiting for us.

"I thought we were supposed to stay separated," Lattimore said.

Dacoolah was sitting on a box. She had changed her dress and fixed her hair a little and looked a lot better. "Circumstances have changed," she said. "I have to talk to you."

"If you're worried, we're leaving in the morning," I said. "We could even leave tonight."

"It didn't work," Lattimore explained.

"Calm down," Dacoolah said. "I'm not kicking you out. I'm just getting interested." She held up a newspaper. "I had no idea what you two had been up to. You've got half New England up in arms."

She spread the newspaper out. It was called the *Taddington Enquirer,* and there were a whole bunch of stories on the front page that were connected with us. "Horses Stampeded Out of Camp Downing"; "Are Heroin Pushers Loose in Sackville County?"; "Hospital Officials Welcome Two Connolly Kids"; "Schreckers Threatened by Extortionists."

We started to read them, but Dacoolah said, "You can look at your press clippings later. We have more important things to talk about now." We quit reading and she went on. "You said earlier you left a lot of false trails and I believed you, I really did, because I could see even then that you were boys of some inventiveness. But I never expected anything like this." She pointed to the newspaper. "False trails! You've laid out supertrails . . . no, that's not right. Intercontinental trails . . . no . . . "

"Superhighways," Lattimore said.

"That's it. Superhighways of falseness. I've never heard of so much confusion being sown by so few in such a short time. Ten grown men couldn't have done it! You have my admiration on the technical side alone, to say nothing of the other, the . . . um, ethical issue. But you may need help from now on, and that's why I'm here now. I'm throwing in with you. It's the least I can do, to put my money where my admiration is. No, I have that wrong . . . should say to put my admiration where your money is."

167

She talked kind of like any other old New Englander —I mean, her accent and the words she used and the way she rambled around—but the sense was different.

"That's nice of you, Dacoolah," Lattimore said. "It's more than nice, it's great. But I don't see how any of us can do anything now." And he told her how Campbell had acted.

Dacoolah took all that in, and then she wanted to hear everything that had happened at Camp Downing, and we told her. She listened and didn't say a word, but when we got to some of the things Campbell had told us about the Schreckers and how they had worked on him and why, her hands tightened up where she had them laced together until you could see the knuckles turn white. But she didn't say anything until we'd finished.

Then she reached down and got a bottle of gin and a glass that she had by the side of the box and poured herself a drink and stood up and drank it. Then she poured another one and started walking around, holding it in her hand. She left the bottle on the box.

You could tell she was walking around to gather her thoughts for a speech, and that the gin was supposed to make it come out smooth. Dad does that, too, but he's not a real actor so the result is never as good.

It took a while, but she was finally ready.

"There's so much you should know," she began, "and I don't know if I can explain it so you can *see* it. The main thing is that you don't lose heart. We aren't finished yet. But you have to understand exactly what

168

we're up against in the Schreckers. And how they get away with what they do. To understand them, though, you have to understand Taddington first. And then all of New England and the East, and finally the whole country. A large order."

She walked around and thought about that.

"New England! I noticed that both of you were laughing at New England when you were telling me about Tommy Campbell and the Schreckers—yes, you were—and I guess we are funny. But this could have happened in the Pacific Northwest or the Middle West or anywhere else in the United States—including Palm Beach, Ox—yes, it could. It might have looked a little different, and it might have taken longer and so on, but it could have happened. Things like it are happening all over America all the time.

"I know about that because I'm caught between two worlds. New England by birth, the South by profession. Six years ago, I left the stage—let's be truthful, I was washed up—and returned to Taddington, and all the old charm and horror of New England came rushing back and I was part of it again. But not entirely, because the other world could not be altogether crowded out. Now I am never sure what I am—is it any wonder I call my book *Between Two Worlds*?

"That's beside the point . . . or is it? Anyhow, what is happening here now makes such an impression because Taddington is the kind of place it is. Thirty years ago, it was still a sleepy New England town. A pretty big one, with almost fifteen thousand people, but still a town. Practically everyone who lived here was a native Vermonter. Then the outsiders started coming in."

She explained how it had happened. First the people with some money and position, like the Schreckers, getting away from the commuter belt around New York. Then the next bunch, with a little less money, and each bunch after that with much less. "Now there are thirty thousand people here and half of them are outsiders. Most of them have more money than we do, and they've taken over. The ones without money have taken over our jobs. They even run barber shops. It's their town now—we're completely colonized.

"You ask why the natives don't do something about it? What can we do? This is a free country, isn't it? No, don't answer that . . . but isn't it, in the simple sense that you can live where you want? If a lot of outsiders choose to live in Taddington, the natives can't fight them. And besides, the natives all make money out of it, so the arrangement is fine with them.

"Anyhow, that's the way it is, and the Schreckers are right at the top of the heap. They're like the British viceroy used to be in India. What they want is what everyone in Taddington finds out he'd better want, too. Including the district attorney, the judges . . . everyone."

She poured herself another drink.

"Campbell told us about that," Lattimore said. "About how no one can sue because the Schreckers own all the lawyers."

170

"Yes, I'm sure," Dacoolah said. "Yes, that explains their power here. But what about Boston, you ask. What about New York? How does their influence extend to the big cities?" She leaned forward and said very softly, "It's because they're mad."

We didn't say anything and she went on. "You boys are confused because on the one hand the Schreckers seem to be knowing and clever and just straight crooks. And then on the other they seem to be quite crazy, believing what they say. And you wonder how they can be crooks and crazy at the same time. Isn't that right? Don't you wonder that?"

We both nodded. She was right, that was what had both of us going.

"The answer is in Shakespeare!" she cried. She had both arms stretched out and her face turned up and she looked like some kind of prophet. "The incomparable Hamlet was conscious of what he was doing and mad at one and the same time—the first modern man. It's old-fashioned to think people have to be one way or the other. They can be all ways at once. And the more they are that way, the stronger they are. It fascinates people. People *think* they are drawn to the Schreckers because he's the famous cancer researcher and she's the famous ceramic designer. Scientists, writers, artists, bankers, lawyers—all come to Pilgrim's Knob when they're asked to Schrecker parties. 'Oh, the Schreckers are so talented, so charming, such fun,' they say. But that's not it at all. It's because they're mad, several people at once. How else could they have be-

171

come the shining examples of everything they are not? They are considered so lovely—just the opposite of what they really are. You know, Schrecker insists Mrs. S. is a saint and has written a pamphlet to prove it. He's also written an inspirational book for his grandchildren, all about how the right spirit can defeat the devil.

"When they bought the old Burnside place and moved in, I met them, of course, and put them down immediately as joke people. He pompous and silly and quite insecure, she mealy-mouthed and deceitful. And on top of that, great bores. They renamed the place Pilgrim's Knob and built that chapel and I was sure they were just joke people and nothing else. But I was wrong. They were only jokes on one level. On another they were strong, sinister, *dramatic* figures . . . yes, dramatic.

"They took me up and I thought it was because I was a 'figure' to them—the old actress with a fund of memories and anecdotes. And I took the time to amuse them because I thought they were pathetic, like shut-ins. I had no idea *they* were doing the condescending, that I was only performing in *their* play. . . .

"The things that have gone on at that place! The wild fights, the drunken shouts, the overt brutality. Most of it played as comedy, like the surrealistic marriages at their chapel."

Dacoolah had another drink. Her eyes were shining and her skin looked wet, too. She was relaxed in one way and tense in another. She was using big words, and

I didn't understand a lot of them, even if Lattimore did, but we couldn't miss the sense. And the way she could make us *see* everything. She was a real actress and we couldn't stop listening to her and watching her.

"They held those marriages on summer afternoons —marvelous confusions of intent and mood. The dithering bishop, the mismatched couples, the wildly assorted people—it always looked like the finale of some contemporary musical, with the bankers and museum directors peeling off their ties and the hippies clapping them on the back . . . they were all such marvelous parody people.

"Parody! That's the word for the Schreckers. In everything they do, the parodies are pushed to the ultimate. They make a joke out of everything. And everyone. Of themselves most of all, naturally."

She had another drink, and by that time she was really glowing. "But the one thing I must give them is that they are *great theater*. Don't they have to be, considering that they are so Shakespearean? Little people may say they have the blackmail of madness, because a mad person who is not locked up has such a strong position. Others know they're mad, but only subconsciously, so they can't do anything about it. When Dr. Schrecker gives them an order, they're so terrified they obey without question. . . . But those are only little people who say that about blackmail, little people who have no feeling for great art.

"Ah, the Schreckers! Mad parodies let loose on a

naïve America that knows all about licensed madness in ancient Rome and Czarist Russia, but can't see it under its own nose. The little people think the old gods are dead, that people like Nero and Rasputin are gone forever. But they are wrong, the old gods never die. They rise again—in the Schreckers! What theater! What I would give to play Mrs. S. in Ibsen's version! The parts I've lost . . . sheer carelessness. The roles that have been taken from me! Weren't Hitler and Stalin more interesting than the man down the block? We only get what we deserve, and the Schreckers are certainly Divine retribution in one form or another.

"What Tommy Campbell tells you is true. They sincerely believe they're decent people. How could they be mad—and great—if they didn't believe that? It's the final proof of their madness. When they go down to Boston and plot with the trust officer they *think* they're acting in Tommy's interests. They really do. At least part of the time. Like all great actors, half in and half out of character.

"That's what you're up against, you two from the audience. That's why you can't win. If they were conscious crooks you *might* win. But you can't beat madness. You can't beat art. You can't beat greatness. You can't beat Shakespeare. You can't beat the theater."

She was staggering by then and we helped her onto the box.

"Gimme a drink," she said. Lattimore didn't want to, but I've had to live around too many drinkers to argue. I poured her a good strong one.

She held it out. "Here's to the Schreckers," she said. "Greatest actors in the world." Then she drank it down and shuddered a while.

Lattimore was sore by that time. "I thought you were on our side," he said.

"Always on the side of art," she muttered, and then hiccuped. "Art always wins. Works in mysterious ways. Uses the wicked for its own ends. Read Shaw. The Life Force . . . I was great, but I was never that great. Ruined life. You say the Schreckers are brutal, and that's true, but if the audience can't see madness they will always find ways of calling the brutality something else. Kindness. Art protects its own." She stood up, weaving a little, but more in control.

"Remember art," she said. "Remember Dacoolah, who serves art. No matter what form it comes in. Forget the little moralities. See the big picture. Good night."

What she was saying sounded wild, but she was almost back to normal again. When she walked out of the barn she was walking fairly straight, and she only hiccuped once.

"What a mess she turned out to be," Lattimore said. He was really sore.

"She was only tight," I said. "That's just the way it took her."

"Why, she ended up saying the Schreckers are wonderful," he said.

"I don't think she meant it," I told him.

"How can you be so dumb? I thought you were smart and now you . . . "

175

"I think the Schreckers really upset her. I think she can't stand the way they are and what they get away with. It hurts her so much that she has to twist it around and around inside herself and make it come out backward. I've seen a lot of people do that."

"I haven't," Lattimore said.

"Well, as you say yourself, you've led a sheltered life. When people are in pain they'll say anything."

Lattimore opened his mouth to say something more, and then shut it. I was just as glad, because it was almost midnight and I was still plenty tired from the night before. And plenty sore. I mean physically, from that horse, not in the way Lattimore was.

We turned in without another word.

16

WHEN WE WOKE UP the next morning we lay around and talked. Especially about Dacoolah, and we wondered if we'd be welcome if we showed up at the house. While we were thinking that over, the barn door opened and Dacoolah came in. She was completely sobered up and fairly neat.

"How about some breakfast?" she asked us. "I'll give you fifteen minutes to get ready."

She didn't act like she was embarrassed by anything that had happened.

As soon as she said that, she turned around and left. We pulled ourselves together and picked the hay off each other and brushed up and went along to the house. We came in at the front and worked back to the kitchen, and when we got there I almost fell over because there really was a good breakfast ready. She'd pulled the papers down to one end of the table, and on the bare spot were places for Lattimore and me and a stack of pancakes and sausages. Of course, Dacoolah wasn't such a great cook, and everything was a little overdone or underdone, but for her to have gone to all that trouble meant a lot more than if a good cook had done it.

We pitched right in and cleaned everything up. Even Lattimore was hungry. When we finished, Dacoolah said, "I'm not going to discuss last night—or apologize for it—except to say that even if much of what I said was true, my eulogy of the Schreckers wasn't. They may be the winners, but I'm as sorry about that as you are."

We said we understood, but she looked sort of unhappy, so we started cheering her up a little, talking about the parts of the summer that had been fun. We told her all about Camp Downing and the Skipper and Klondike and things like that. And how we slipped all the horses out and ran into the Connollys. It took some doing to make Dacoolah laugh, but when she started she couldn't stop. At first she was covering her bad teeth with her hand when she laughed, but after a while she didn't care and just opened her mouth and let go.

Then Lattimore showed her how to talk Schrecker talk, and they did that together for a while. Lattimore was Mrs. Schrecker and Dacoolah was the mad doctor and they were good. It's better with two people. Especially when one of them is a real actress. It wasn't long before she was quicker than Lattimore.

When they got tired of that they wrote the Schreckers some postcards.

Then that sort of wound down and we were all left looking at each other.

Dacoolah finally said, "I know what you're thinking —that there must be some way. But there isn't. Look, I have a few friends here—the clerk of the court, a lawyer, and the owner of a hardware store. The first two are natives and the last is originally from New Jersey, but a trustworthy man. I could get them up here and tell them the whole story and they would probably be indignant enough to go out and try to do something about it. They'd try to persuade some other people to come in with them and build public pressure against the Schreckers. To the point where the law would move, either through a judge issuing some order, or through the police."

"That doesn't sound too bad," Lattimore said.

"But it wouldn't work," Dacoolah said. "They'd all get turned down. I can just see Sam White—he's the one who owns the hardware store—coming out here to tell me that. 'I can't do a thing,' he'd say."

"Wouldn't he tell you why?" Lattimore asked her.

"Oh, sure," Dacoolah said, "but what would that mean?"

"I'd still like to know why," Lattimore said.

"All right," she said, "you shall hear it in his own

words." She leaned forward and lowered her voice and started in as Sam White. " 'Jim Simmons, Bill Irving, Charley Flagler, the whole crowd I play poker with, go to Beaver Lake with, guys I always thought were my friends, saw things the way I do, had the same idea of ordinary morality . . . but, boy, how you get to know people when the chips are down. I didn't know those guys at all, it turns out. Not one of them will do a thing. What do you think of that?' "

I almost clapped, she could imitate that Sam White so well. She was as good as Jonathan Winters with those small-town Americans.

"What reasons do they give?" Dacoolah asked in her normal voice, as though Sam White was there in front of her, and then she was him again, answering. " 'You can't find out. Not the real reasons. They mutter something about kids exaggerating things. They won't buy the idea that the Schreckers are trying to drive a kid crazy for his trust fund. It has to be because they respect the Schreckers or they're afraid of them or something like that.' "

She stopped then.

"I guess you're right," Lattimore said.

"Control is control," Dacoolah said. "When they say the Schreckers control this town, they mean *control*."

"What if we took it higher?" Lattimore asked her. "To the attorney general. Even to the governor."

"It wouldn't do any good," I said.

"I was just kidding myself," Lattimore said. "Of

course, the higher you go, the more power the Schreck-ers have. Dacoolah was right last night. And again today. Let's take our licking and not make it worse."

"I'm very sorry," Dacoolah said, and she wasn't acting.

"We'd better get out of here," I told Lattimore. "All those newspapers Dacoolah showed us. They're looking for us everywhere now. And Campbell may talk. If we stay we're going to be caught."

"I'm afraid that's true," Dacoolah said. "But where can you go?"

"Home, I guess," Lattimore said.

"How will you get there?"

"Plane, I guess."

"From where?"

"Boston."

"How will you get to Boston?" You sort of had the idea that she was asking all those questions so she wouldn't have to think about the rest of it. I didn't blame her, because I didn't want to think about it either.

"I'll drive you," Dacoolah said. "I have an old truck —I call it Doug Fairbanks."

"No, it's too far," Lattimore said. "And if they miss you around here, they'll be suspicious. As you said, they could make it tough on you for helping us. Just drive us across the state line, into Massachusetts. Then we can get a train or a bus to Boston."

She thought that was a good idea, and we went out to the barn and got our stuff while she poured some gas in Doug Fairbanks. That was some pickup truck, about fifty years old, but very frisky for its age. It was what they call a Model T, almost as small as a toy car, and it jumped and bucked instead of running like any other car or pickup I ever saw. She called it Doug Fairbanks because there was once a famous actor by that name who jumped around a lot in his films. She was in a movie with him when she was young. I think I've seen him a few times myself on the Late Show.

She kept Doug in a little shed off the barn, and she had so much trouble backing out that Lattimore had to get in and do it for her. Then she took the wheel and Lattimore and I squeezed in beside her, and we started off. It was like riding Klondike.

Even in Doug it didn't take long to drive into Massachusetts, because Taddington is only about thirty miles north of the state line. I was afraid there'd be a roadblock or something, but there wasn't.

Dacoolah had brought along a bottle of gin, and took a nip once in a while, but it seemed to help her driving instead of the other way around, so we didn't mind. She was pretty quiet when we started, but after a few nips she began to talk again.

"I'm such a fool," she said. "I always think I have to give a performance if I'm paid. I suppose that explains the show I put on last night." We must have looked sort of confused, because then she said, "I don't mean the hundred dollars. That was only money. I'd been paid in a different coin. It isn't often that one meets real people any more. Of any age."

No one said anything to that, and she went on. "Yesterday I did find out a few things about this Tommy Campbell's trust fund from my lawyer friend. It's in Boston at the New England Exchange Bank and the Schreckers are already milking it. The capital is about ten million, and the annual income almost half a million. Five hundred thousand a year! Of course, taxes eat up most of that, but there's still about a hundred thousand net each year, and the Schreckers are taking the lion's share of that for 'Tommy's support.' Which includes, naturally, paying off a lot of people in Taddington, among them Stella Smith, the judge who issued the original custody order. So there's actually not much left for the Schreckers themselves now. But if they can get Tommy into a sanitarium, they'll eventually wind up with all the capital. Less only the chunk they'll have to pay the bank. Let's say one quarter. Even I, who am slow at figures, can see that amounts to over seven million. Can you imagine it? And people ask, 'Why are they doing it?' They're doing it for the money. Right, Doug?" And she pushed down on the gas and old Doug jumped around like he was agreeing and she had another drink.

About ten miles past the state line we came into a town called Mallaby and pulled up at the railroad station there.

"You can get a train to Boston in a few hours," Dacoolah said.

We got out and said good-bye to her. She didn't say much of anything, and when she did her voice sounded funny. Her eyes were funny, too. It was more than the gin, because she hadn't had that much. It was almost as if she didn't want to look at us.

"I'll always remember you boys," she said just before she left.

"Same here," Lattimore said. "You were good to us. Don't forget to mail the postcards. We'll keep making them sore if we can't do anything else. I'll send another batch from Boston."

"I won't forget," Dacoolah said, and she started Doug up and off they went, bucking and lurching away.

It was about three then, and we went into the little station and found out that the next train to Boston was at six.

We went back outside and I said, "We can't just sit around here until six."

"What do you suggest?"

"There must be an airport. Let's fly to Boston. We've got plenty of money."

"I don't think there are any scheduled flights out of a place this small."

"We'll charter a plane."

His eyes bugged out. "Won't that leave a pretty big trail?"

"What if it does? I'm tired of doing things the uncomfortable way. Let's go out with a splash."

So we found a taxi driver who was about ninety years old and told him to take us to the nearest airport. He was one of those real New Englanders who say "Eh?" and put a hand behind their ears to hear you, and it took him a long time to get it. The idea of two kids taking a taxi to the airport, which was about ten miles away, was almost too much for him. I had to tell him a big story about my uncle dying of gangrene in Washington, D.C., and we had to get there in a hurry. Finally he let us in his taxi and started off.

The airport was a little place, but there was an office there and a couple of planes for charter. I told the pilot the same story and dressed it up a little. I could see Lattimore ready to burst out laughing, but I knew what I was doing. I can't do any of the stuff he can do, but I'm good at telling a story that sounds pathetic.

"It'll cost you," the pilot said. "About a hundred and twenty."

"My aunt sent plenty of money," I told him. "I can pay you in advance if you want."

"Give me fifty now and the rest when we get to Boston," he said.

We piled into the plane, one of those little Piper Aztecs, and took off. When Lattimore was sure the pilot couldn't hear him, he said to me, "Ox, you know how to travel."

"I learned it from Dad," I said.

We were in Boston in about an hour, and I paid off the pilot and told him we'd be catching the first flight for Washington. He said he hoped my uncle would recover, but I told him it looked pretty bad.

Then we walked through the airport, carrying our suitcases, and caught a taxi into Boston.

185

"Where to, Chief?" the taxi driver asked.

"The Ritz," Lattimore said. "I'm learning," he whispered to me.

He was a little nervous about how we were going to handle it at the Ritz, but I told him it would be easy and it was. I went to the desk and asked for a reservation in the name of Swanson. When the clerk said there wasn't one, I let my eyes get sort of wet and confused and said, "But my grandmother was supposed to be meeting us here, and she said she'd reserve a room for her and one for me and my brother."

"Nothing here," he said. "But we can give you a room."

"I'll take it. Maybe I better take two, so Granny will have one when she gets here." I knew there had to be a room in an adult's name, whether the adult ever showed up or not. They never let two kids stay in an expensive hotel on their own.

"I can give you two adjoining double rooms with baths," he said. "What is the full name?"

"Mrs. Abigail Swanson, 613 Letcher Street, Bar Harbor, Maine." I'd been practicing that name and address all the way in from the airport, putting it together from New England names that Lattimore gave me. It was his idea to do it all under Swanson. "Just for old time's sake," he said. We were William Swanson and George Swanson.

"You're sure your grandmother will show up?" the clerk asked. "These rooms are over forty dollars a day each."

I could tell he was worried about the money, and I

186

had a hundred ready in my hand. "She sent us plenty of money," I said. "I can give you a deposit."

After he saw the hundred there was no trouble at all.

When we got upstairs we took baths and changed into what were supposed to be our good clothes. We had them pressed first, and we didn't look too bad.

Mine smelled a little funny, because I'd packed the rest of the food we had in the barn in with my clothes.

When Lattimore saw that stuff he put his hand up to his forehead and staggered back. "No, Ox, no," he said. "All those old groceries in the Ritz! The room looks like peace marchers are living here."

"All right, I'll throw it out," I said. And I did. It was all hot and too old anyhow.

Then we went down to the dining room and had two tremendous steaks and everything that went with them, and charged them to the room. Even Lattimore was hungry.

When we were done, we leaned back in our chairs and Lattimore said, "What next, Chief?"

"We'll take a little walk," I said. "But I mean a little one, just enough to settle dinner. Then we'll go to a movie. Then we'll have about fourteen hours of sleep. Then we'll see."

"You're a planner," Lattimore said.

"We were making a big mistake doing things everybody else's way. Now we'll do them our way. If they work, they work. If they don't, they don't. But we'll have a good time while we're at it, and when the money's gone we'll go home."

"It sounds right to me," he said, and then he went

upstairs to call Anne before we went out.

When he came back he said, "She's sorry about Campbell, but she's pretty impressed with our present setup. Sends her best to you. She's got my mother under control, but barely. They read the papers up there and we're in them, too."

"They don't read them much in Palm Beach," I told him. "And it's pretty far away, anyhow."

"That town has so many advantages," Lattimore said.

So we went out and saw the movie. It was called *Sleuth* and was pretty good for an English movie. Then we came back to the Ritz and had a good sleep.

17

WE SLEPT A LONG TIME, but not fourteen hours. It was about ten or eleven, because we were up at nine.

We had a good breakfast. At least I did. Eggs on pancakes and a triple order of sausages and a lot of toasted muffins and orange juice. We had it in the room, and there were a lot of dishes around when I was done. Lattimore didn't eat much at breakfast. He knocked off some postcards to the Schreckers while I finished up.

He read them all to me and they were pretty good. Except one that said, "A trust fund a day keeps the doctor away." Underneath that it said, "Old New England Proverb."

"Trust funds don't keep him away," I said. "They make him come."

"Not if you give them to him," Lattimore said. "If you give him your trust fund he stays away. In fact, it's the only way to keep him out of the house." Lattimore had an answer for everything. It did sort of make sense when you thought it over, but I still didn't think it was one of his best ones.

Then we talked about trust funds and Lattimore said, "I'd like to see this Hugo Lewis, the one at the bank who's working with the Schreckers."

"I don't think we'll be able to do anything with him," I said.

"I'm not going to try anything," Lattimore said. "I just want to have a look at him. I want to see with my own eyes the kind of person who'll do what all these people have been doing."

"It's all right with me," I said. "But won't we be spotted then?"

"We'll use fake names. I'll be Campbell's cousin, Jack Campbell, and you'll be *my* cousin, Angus Campbell. We're all Scots and we stick together."

"Where are we from?"

"I'm from Maryland and you're from . . . Virginia."

"But I don't have a southern accent."

"You go north to school. We both go to Choate."

"It won't work," I said. "A bank officer won't talk about trust funds to two kids."

"Sure he will," Lattimore said. "Older people fall all over themselves for kids now."

"Not the ones I know."

190

"Those are Palm Beach oldies. In the rest of the country they're always 'learning from the young.' It's the latest thing. Even the newspapers are full of it. Kids can push anyone around."

"We don't seem to be doing so well with the Schreckers."

"Well, there have to be exceptions. Anyhow, those two are more like super-kids than adults."

"You have an answer for everything," I said. He did, too.

"Besides," he said, "we're not exactly little kids. I'm as big as most men and you're a lot bigger. We're borderline kids. We're practically young adults, and they have even more pull than kids."

"You're convincing me," I said.

"And here's the clincher. The last thing Dacoolah told us about was how much this trust fund has in it and where it is. I don't think she did that by accident. She was giving us a lead. And I think she has some sort of magic to her. Like an old sorceress or a witch."

"I'm sold," I said.

We went out and took a taxi to the New England Exchange Bank. It was a huge place and I was a little nervous when we went in. I can handle hotels and airports, but I'm not too good with banks. It's just the other way with Lattimore.

"Why are we here?" I asked him as we went in.

"We're worried about Cousin Tommy. Leave it to me."

I did, and I have to say he handled it just right. We

were in the bank by then, and he didn't rush up to a teller or a guard or anything. He just stood there and I stood with him, and after a couple of minutes a guard came up and asked what we wanted.

"We want to see Mr. Hugo Lewis," Lattimore said.

"Mr. Lewis—he's head of the trust department. Do you have an appointment?"

"No."

"What do you want to see him about?"

"We'll discuss that with him," Lattimore said.

The guard didn't like that, but you could see he'd found out Lattimore was a rich kid and couldn't exactly be handled like other kids.

"I'll take you to Mr. O'Keefe," the guard said, and we went with him to a man who had a desk behind a railing. He was young and had long hair and bangs and asked us what we wanted to see Mr. Lewis about. When Lattimore gave him the same answer he'd given the guard, Mr. O'Keefe shook his head and said he'd have to know more because Mr. Lewis was such a busy man and so important.

Lattimore lowered his voice and said, "Just tell him we went to see him about Tommy Campbell. We're his cousins. I can guarantee he'll see us then."

Mr. O'Keefe acted as though he didn't believe it, but he phoned up to Mr. Lewis's office and got his secretary and asked to speak to Mr. Lewis, and when he got him he said, "There are two boys here who say they want to see you, something about a Tommy Campbell. They're cousins of his." He listened for a minute and then he put the phone down and gave us a big friendly smile and said, "You can go right up."

"I told you," Lattimore said, and we moved off to the elevators before Mr. O'Keefe could say anything to that. Lattimore always liked to have the last word, and he usually did. This time he was giving it to me as well as to Mr. O'Keefe.

"But I knew it was a cinch," he told me later. "There Mr. Lewis was, sitting up there feeling as guilty as anything about what the Schreckers and he were doing to that fund—and going to do—and someone phones up to say the victim's cousins are there. He *had* to find out what we knew. Not only for himself but for the S.'s. If he'd refused to see us they would have been on his neck for not investigating every lead. No, when you think about it, how could he *not* have seen us? He couldn't."

We got off at the third floor, and there was a sign on a big door made out of expensive wood: *Hugo T. S. Lewis, Senior Vice President and Executive Officer, Trust Department.* His secretary sent us right in.

Mr. Lewis had an office suite all to himself, with plenty of carpets and paintings on the walls. He walked around from behind his desk to shake hands with us. He wasn't a bad-looking man, and he was pretty pleasant. His hair was shorter than normal.

"Well, boys," he said. "What can I do for you?"

He didn't ask our names, so Lattimore told him. He was Jack Campbell and I was Angus Campbell, and he was from Maryland and I was from Virginia, just the way he had said. Then he got up steam and said we were passing through Boston on our way to Maine, where his grandmother had a summer place, and she had asked us to call Tommy at the Schreckers. And we'd called him and he'd said he was pretty unhappy there, and we'd told him we were sorry to hear that and we asked him if there was anything we could do. And he said maybe we could ask Mr. Lewis to help him, because Mr. Lewis was such a nice man. So that was why we were here. Lattimore did it just right, not too fast and not too slow, and very sincere.

When he finished Mr. Lewis said, "I didn't know Tommy had a cousin named Jack. But that's beside the point, I suppose. Yes, I know Tommy *says* he's unhappy. But the doctors claim he's not himself, so how do we know whether he's telling the truth or not? The Schreckers are very nice people, and it's just impossible to believe what Tommy says against them."

"I don't agree with you," Lattimore said. "I don't think the Schreckers are nice people."

"On what do you base that?"

"Well, my grandmother hired a private detective to investigate them. In his report he said a lot of people in Taddington told him they weren't nice, and that they were after Tommy's trust fund, the one that's here in this bank."

"That's absurd," Mr. Lewis said.

"Mr. Lewis, if Tommy cracked up completely—if he had to go into a sanitarium or something—what would happen to that fund?"

"I don't really see why I should tell you."

"Why not?"

"Frankly, it's none of your business."

"I see," Lattimore said. He didn't make a fuss, but looked at me as if he was some sort of expert and he was saying, "Hmmmmmm, just as I thought."

"What do you see?" Mr. Lewis asked Lattimore. That look had upset him.

"Well, if you won't tell me, then I have to believe Tommy when he says the Schreckers will benefit, the way they already have."

"What do you mean—the way they already have?"

"They get a lot of the income for his 'support' now, don't they?"

"They get a reasonable amount."

"How much is that?"

"Again, that's none of your business."

Then Lattimore dropped the politeness. "Listen, Mr. Lewis," he said, "I may be only a kid, but I know there's something fishy here. There's some way the Schreckers have figured out to get all that money. Don't ask me how—that's your department. When Campbell—Cousin Tommy—is finally locked up as a permanent nut, then I suppose the bank will make them co-trustees or whatever they call it. They'll end up with full control of everything."

"You're as wild as Tommy," Mr. Lewis said. Behind him were some framed photographs. One was of a bunch of officers in Navy uniforms, I guess from the last World War. And two or three of his wife and grown children.

"The Schreckers are maniacs," Lattimore was saying. "I've seen him twist a woman's wrist to make her give in to him." Mr. Lewis started to say something, but Lattimore kept going. "Even so, I'm not here to talk about the Schreckers. I know all about them. What I'm here for is to see with my own eyes what kind of man you are to play along with them. Why do you do it, Mr. Lewis? Do they pay you off or is it because you think they're so wonderful?"

Mr. Lewis stood up then and he was very sore all of a sudden.

"If you were a man I'd throw you out of my office," he said. "As it is, I'll only ask you to leave."

"I've been looking at your photographs," I said. "What would all those men you knew in the war think of you if they knew what you'd done against a defenseless kid? And your wife and children—what would they think?"

"You can't talk that way to me," he said, and he came around the corner of his desk at me.

"You touch him and you're in trouble," Lattimore said quietly, and Mr. Lewis stopped. "And I don't mean only for striking a minor, either. You may not have noticed, but Angus is about twice as big as you are and there's plenty of muscle under that flab. You'd probably end up stuffed in your own wastebasket."

"I won't touch either of you," Mr. Lewis said, with his voice trembling. "But if you aren't out of this office in the next ten seconds and out of the building a minute after that, I'll call the guards and they'll throw you out."

196

"You go ahead and do that," Lattimore said, "and the newspapers will have a great time. We came here with a reporter and a photographer. They're waiting downstairs for any fireworks."

Mr. Lewis just stared at us, and then he went back and sat down behind his desk.

"You're afraid of publicity, aren't you!" Lattimore blazed at him. "Because you know what you're doing is wrong! You're helping the Schreckers kill a kid to get money. You don't think of it that way, maybe, but that's what it is. I don't know what you get out of it—money for yourself or for the bank, or just the thrill of working for the Schreckers. But whatever you get, it's not enough for what you're doing."

Mr. Lewis jumped up and now his eyes were really wild. "If you won't leave my office, I'll leave it," he yelped. "I'll go downstairs and arrange for you to be taken out a side door. No reporters . . . "

He was running for the door and talking to himself. When he was gone, Lattimore looked at me and shrugged his shoulders. "They're so smooth," he said. "Until they get excited."

We walked out past the secretary, who was staring at us, and took the elevator down. When we stepped out on the ground floor we saw a bunch of guards going through a door at the back of the main lobby and up some stairs. Mr. Lewis was with them, still wild.

We walked out the front door and no one followed us.

I needed a snack so we stopped in a delicatessen. I had a pretty good pastrami sandwich and a large order of potato salad. Lattimore didn't have anything.

"Wasn't that something," he said finally.

"Yes, but I don't know what it means."

"If it doesn't mean anything else, it means that no one sees what's under their noses. Is this whole country crazy?"

"Do you want an honest answer?"

"No."

I was glad he didn't, because my mouth was full of pastrami.

"I'll tell you what I want to do," Lattimore said. "I want to see this Dr. Foster."

"Aw, come on. Haven't you had enough?"

"Hi can't get henough," he said in Cockney. "Hi'm a glutton for punishment, Hi ham."

So we got a taxi and went all the way out to Cambridge, which was about seven miles away, to see Dr. Foster at his child psychology clinic at Harvard. There were a lot of hippies lying around on the grass outside.

"Same story?" I asked Lattimore. "Campbell cousins and the rest?"

"Same story," Lattimore said.

And it worked the same way. The secretary wouldn't let us in, and then she called Dr. Foster and said some cousins of Tommy Campbell's were out in front, and he said to send them right in.

I could see why Campbell had liked him. He didn't try to impress on you how important he was, although you could tell from the way the place was set up that he had to be.

And he really was the kind of adult that Lattimore had been talking about—the kind who has more time and respect for kids than for most other adults. Of course, that's time and respect for the regular kid who has "interesting" problems and solutions—he didn't know until too late that Lattimore and I didn't make the grade.

Lattimore gave him the same stuff about how worried we were over Cousin Tommy, and how he hated the Schreckers and said they were after his trust fund, and Dr. Foster said, "He told me all that, and I asked him *why*. That's still my question."

"He says they're just naturally piggy," Lattimore said. "Aren't there people like that?"

Dr. Foster laughed and said, "Yes, there are. But I'm not sure the Schreckers qualify. You know, they're really very nice people."

"No, they're not," Lattimore said. He dropped the act, they way he had in the bank. "They're not nice at all. They're vicious and they're crazy. And you know it. Or you should know it."

"Wait a minute," Dr. Foster said. "You're going too fast for me. Could you say that again?"

"You heard it all," Lattimore said.

"I'm not sure I did," Dr. Foster said. "Did you hear it?" he asked me.

All grown-ups have their game, and that was his. "Sure I heard it, Dr. Foster," I said. "And so did you."

"Now let me see if I have it straight," he said. "The Schreckers are vicious and crazy and after Tommy's money. And I'm supposed to know all this. Right?"

"Right," Lattimore said.

"But how do you know they're vicious and crazy?"

"How do you know a dog is that way?" Lattimore asked. "By looking at him. That's the way anyone knows about the Schreckers, too. Haven't you ever looked at them? I mean, really taken a good look? And listened?"

"I have," Dr. Foster said. "And I'm afraid I still find them very nice people and not at all crazy or vicious. Crazy, incidentally, is not a medical term."

"And do you think Tommy is crazy?" Lattimore asked him. "Or whatever the medical term is?"

"I've never said that," Dr. Foster said. "I think he's depressed and upset about something. My guess is it's because he's lost his parents. I think he has a good chance of getting over the way he feels. But I most emphatically don't think it's caused by the Schreckers."

"I don't see how you can face yourself in the morning," Lattimore said.

"Outside of needing a shave, why do you think that?" Dr. Foster asked him. He was a lot smoother than Mr. Lewis and didn't seem to get mad at anything.

"They're trying to drive Campbell crazy to get his money," Lattimore told him. "Everyone in Taddington knows it, and this Mr. Lewis at the Exchange Bank practically admits it. You're in up to your neck because it all depends on medical opinion. You're the expert, the key person, in something that's worse than a murder. That's why I ask you how you can face yourself in the morning."

That shot finally got home. Dr. Foster fiddled with his pens a minute and when he talked again his voice was different, more serious. "I'm as honest a doctor and psychiatrist as I can be. My opinion in this case is as disinterested as I can make it. I've formed decisions from the medical evidence and nothing else. If you can't believe that . . . "

"That's what you *think* has happened," Lattimore said in an excited way. "And you think that because you're so sure you can't be fooled. But you have been fooled. You've been fooled by people who fool themselves, and then you believe them because you can see they believe what they're doing. You've been had because there's more strangeness and evil in this world than you ever thought of."

There was another long silence. Then Dr. Foster said, "That may be. But in that case there's nothing I can do."

"Why not?" I asked him. "You can unfool yourself. You can wise up."

"Not until I'm sure I've been fooled. And I'm certainly not sure yet."

"I give up," Lattimore said. "He's a nice man, just like Campbell said. But he's got all this training and science and medicine standing between him and seeing what a ditchdigger could see in five seconds. It's too much."

"I'm sorry, boys," Dr. Foster said.

His face was strange when he said that. He seemed so calm, but you could tell that deep down he wanted to explode. I think he would have been better off if he had exploded because he didn't look so good holding it in. He looked sort of half dead.

He walked with us to the door and we left and wandered around Harvard through the hippies until we found a taxi. Then we went back to the Ritz.

"Seen enough?" I asked Lattimore.

"I've seen enough," he said. "I never want to see any more. Ox, it isn't that the Schreckers live to hurt people, whether they know it or not. The really strange thing is that no one notices that they live to hurt people. I'll ask you again. Is this whole country crazy?"

"And I'll ask you again—do you want a straight answer?"

"This time I do."

My mouth was empty, so I gave him one. "Well, everyone reads the papers," I started off, "and the papers are full of this stuff about pollution and overpopulation and the end of the natural resources. And in the papers they say that means the end of the world unless people do something to stop it. They've figured it all out and the end is coming in fifty years at the most. Probably a lot sooner. Everyone reads all that, and then they ask themselves who's going to stop it. The guy who's reading the paper knows *he* isn't, and after a while he figures out that no one else is going to, either. So they all know in their hearts that it isn't going to be stopped. And knowing that drives everyone crazy. They try to act normal, but they can't. It's driving them crazy."

"Who told you all that?"

"What do you mean?"

"You didn't figure that out on your own."

"I figured out some of it."

"Come on, tell me."

"Well, Dad told me most of it. But that doesn't mean it's not right. I trust him on things like that because he's serious about enjoying himself. He says you can't enjoy yourself any more because everyone is crazy and they keep getting in the way. So he sat around until he had the answer to why they were crazy."

"Palm Beach, I love you," Lattimore said. "Out of the mouths of the drunk new-rich comes . . . wisdom."

"You can laugh," I said. "But you asked me and I gave you the answer. And it's the right answer even if it is Dad's. Even if it's the only right thing he ever said."

"I'm not laughing," Lattimore said. "How could I? I knew it was right the minute you said it."

18

WHEN WE GOT BACK to the Ritz we went upstairs and lay around and ordered lunch in the room. Roast lamb and lots of it, with potatoes and peas and plenty of ice cream for dessert. I ate most of it, of course, but Lattimore had a bigger appetite than usual and did his share.

While we were eating, Lattimore said, "Well, I guess that's the end of the party, Ox."

"I guess so," I said.

"We never had a chance," he said. "There was too much against us. We never could get on top of them. In any way."

"We kept trying to talk little people into helping us," I said. "That was the mistake. The only chance we had was to get someone with more influence than the Schreckers. Do you remember talking about how the English shake all over when the lord walks in, and how everyone in New England falls down when the Schreckers walk in? We needed someone with more of that . . . power, or whatever you call it, to sail into Taddington. Or into the bank, or the doctor's office."

"You're absolutely right, Ox. But there ain't no such person. Who has more pull in New England than the Schreckers? No one. Well, unless you make an exception of the Connollys."

"I didn't know they had so much."

"Dear boy, dear sheltered Palm Beach boy. New England is where the Connollys come from. New England is where they built their political base, as it's called. From whence they fanned out and captured the hearts of their countrymen. And a good deal besides. In New England they are supreme."

"Some of them come to Palm Beach every so often," I said. "But they're not so important there."

"It must be the only place they're not," Lattimore said. "Up here they're Olympians. They come down from Parnassus to converse with mere mortals."

"You mean that wild bunch out at the camp is that strong?"

"At the moment their parents are, not them. But when the time comes, they will take their place. America couldn't live without them."

"You really mean they're hotter than the Schreckers, even in Taddington?"

"Of course."

"Then why couldn't we have gotten one of them to go in there?"

"To begin with, they're not exactly noted for doing favors. And in the second place, I don't know any of the older Connollys, and they're the only ones who could help. That bunch at the camp are not yet ready to take their places in public life, as I explained. They're still marinating."

That was a word I'd heard a lot but I'd never gotten around to finding out what it meant, so I asked Lattimore then.

"It means meat that's lying around in vinegar or wine or something—to soften it up."

"Why bother? You don't need to do that to a good steak."

"If you ever ate anything except steak, if you were a gourmet instead of just a huge eater, you'd know that there are other kinds of meat and that things are done to them to improve the taste."

"It sounds to me like cheap meat they're trying to pass off."

We talked around like that, and then the waiter took the table out and I had a little nap while Lattimore worked on his postcards.

When I woke up he read me some of them and they were right up there. He had one that went, "Roses are red, violets are blue, if you don't give Campbell back, we'll trust-fund you." It was signed, "The Connollys."

"After our little chat about them I couldn't resist," he said.

"It's too bad Campbell's name isn't Connolly," I

said. "The rest of the Connollys really would trust-fund the Schreckers then."

"Yes, if the Schreckers had a Connolly under lock and key they wouldn't last long."

"What we should have done was give them one," I said.

"What do you mean?"

"Grabbed one and hauled him over to Pilgrim's Knob and left him tied up over there somewhere and then called the Connollys and said the Schreckers had him. They would have gone to get him, and if you're right that would have been the end of the Schreckers."

Lattimore thought about it for a minute. "It would have been perfect," he said. "It's too bad we didn't think of it sooner."

"That's always the way it is with good ideas," I said. "I remember . . . "

"Wait a minute." He held up his hand. "Why is it too late?"

"Aw, come on, we're not at Downing any more and everyone in Vermont is looking for us and . . . "

"We could go back. We could make a night raid. We could have a Connolly at Pilgrim's Knob by to-morrow."

He got up and walked around the room, waving his arms.

"We'd need a car," I said. "We can't do it with horses this time. And we don't have driver's licenses."

He admitted that was a problem, but said we could figure it out.

"Then how are we going to grab one Connolly?" I

asked him. "They're always together."

"That's something we'll have to figure out. But, Ox, don't you see—this is the plan that's on the right track. Everything else has been wrong because we didn't know the score. The only way to beat the Schreckers is to get someone with a bigger hold over people than they have. That's the Connollys. We've solved it. There are still a lot of problems with the details, and I'll even admit that maybe we can't get on top of those problems, but we've solved it in theory."

The way he said it, it sounded good, but I still didn't think we could pull it off. "It may be solved in theory," I said, "but what about the car? We can't hire a car, because the driver would talk. So what does that leave?"

"I admitted we might not be able to solve the details, but doesn't it mean anything to you that we solved it in theory?"

"Not much," I told him. It didn't, either.

"Don't you Palm Beach people say that money buys anything?" Lattimore asked me. "You seem to have the money. How about paying so much that a driver *would* keep his mouth shut?"

"I don't have that much. And we're spending plenty, too."

"Can't you get some more where that thousand came from?"

"Maybe, but probably not as much as we'd need."

"Couldn't you try?"

"Well . . . "

"Couldn't you? Where did you get it, anyhow?"

208

"My grandmother."

"Is she nice?"

"She's . . . she's different. It would take too long to explain."

"Well, can't you try her?"

"My rule is never ask anyone in my family for anything. If they give you something, take it. But never ask."

"All right," Lattimore said, and slumped down on a bed.

I didn't say anything for about five minutes, thinking it over, and then I said, "I told you my rule was not to ask. I never said I wouldn't break the rule."

Lattimore jumped off the bed. "You mean you'll do it?"

"I'll try."

So I called my grandmother in New York and she said hello, and I put it to her. I thought there was no point in beating around the bush.

"Granma," I said, "I need a lot of money."

"How much?"

"Plenty. Let's say five thousand."

"That is a lot of money. Is it for a girl?"

"No, it's to do something for a boy who's in real trouble."

"At that price he must be in real trouble. Is it for his girl?"

"No, he's in trouble on his own."

She was quiet for a minute. Then she asked, "Ox, is it *interesting* trouble?"

"It couldn't be more interesting," I said.

"Then I'm for it," she said. "But I have to get something for my money. I need to have some fun, too. So I'll bring the money up myself and you can tell me all about it. Are you still at that camp?"

"No, I'm in Boston. At the Ritz."

"You travel in style, boy. Book me a room. I'll be there in five hours. About eight o'clock."

"I've already got one for you. But it's in the name of Swanson. You're still my grandmother, but your name is Mrs. Abigail Swanson."

"How can I be your grandmother if my name is Abigail Swanson?"

"My name is Swanson, too."

"It sounds better all the time," she said.

"I'll meet your plane," I told her.

"What do you think I learned to drive racing cars for?" she asked me. "I never travel any other way."

"Don't say anything to Dad or anyone else," I told her.

"Don't worry," she said.

I hung up, and Lattimore said, "Just this end of that conversation was something."

I told him what she'd said and that she was coming and that she'd have the money, and he shook his head the way he always did when he thought about Palm Beach and said, "You people! It's as different as Mars."

Then we started planning how we were going to grab the Connolly.

"There should be three of us," Lattimore said. "Two isn't enough."

"It isn't easy to find a kid who'd go along with something like this."

"I know it," Lattimore said. "And he'd have to be tough, too. Even mean, meaner than we are. You're awfully strong, and I'm not so weak myself, and we have enough brains—I hope. But we need that meanness for an emergency."

"Someone like Dale Tifton," I said.

"I was thinking about him," Lattimore said. "I had a look at him in Philadelphia last year, remember. That's one mean kid."

"Well, you can forget him," I said. "He's *too* mean. And besides, I don't have any idea where you can get hold of him."

Dale is my age and he was in the first story I told, and I explained about him then. How his great-grandmother was Holly Tifton, the most famous hostess Palm Beach ever had. She built Kail, the biggest house ever built in Palm Beach, and there've been some monsters. That was years ago, and it's torn down now and there are about fifty houses on the same amount of ground. Once she was the richest woman in America, and her grandson, Neil, is still head of American Cynadine. But his brother, Carl, Dale's father, is something else. He has two houses in Palm Beach, but they're completely gone to pieces and he's drunk all the time. He weighs about four hundred pounds and doesn't do anything but drink. He was married a lot and Dale ended up living with his mother after his parents were divorced. But she was never around, and he had a tough time. Palm Beach home life is not for kids—look at my own—but Dale's was in a class by itself. It made him so mean they couldn't put him in schools or anything.

In the first story I told how he ran away and got into the movies. He was good in the one movie he made, about Jiminy Crockett's life story, but he didn't make any more because his father got him back to Palm Beach. Since then it's always the same thing. He runs away and then he gets caught.

I explained to Lattimore that you never knew where Dale was.

"You could try to call him," Lattimore said. "He's just what we want."

"I'm not sure we could control him if we got him," I said.

"What about using money?"

"Well, yes, he's always broke."

"If we offered him, say, five hundred and expenses, and didn't pay him until it was over . . . how about that?"

"It might work."

"I think it's worth a try."

It made sense—as much as anything did—and I started calling Dale in Palm Beach. I got the numbers from Information. He wasn't at his mother's. I didn't get her, but some friend of hers said he hadn't been there for two weeks. Neither had she. Then I tried his father's and got Mr. Tifton himself. It was direct dialing, so I pretended I was a kid named Grover calling right from Palm Beach.

Mr. Tifton yelled on the phone and cursed Dale up and down, and then cursed me, but he finally told me Dale was in Chicago, staying with some Tiftons there. I kept talking and finally got the name, Mrs. Lorillard Tifton.

Then I gave that to the operator, and she looked up the number in Chicago and I called. A butler answered and said he'd see if Dale was in. He didn't sound too happy about having Dale there.

When Dale said hello, I said, "This is Ox. I'm in Boston and I need your help to do something. If you get on the next plane I'll pay all your expenses and give you five hundred. It won't be for more than a couple of days." I thought there was no sense in beating around the bush with him, either.

One thing about Dale, nothing ever surprises him. The ordinary kid, even a smart kid like Lattimore, would have started asking questions, but Dale only said, "OK, how do I get the plane ticket?"

I'd already checked on that. "You go to the United desk at O'Hare Airport. They'll have the ticket and a hundred. When you get to Boston, take a taxi to the Ritz. I'm here under the name of Swanson."

"All right," he said. Nothing ever surprises him.

"You have to get here as fast as you can."

"I'll be there on the next plane. Relax."

"Do you have enough to get a taxi to the airport?"

"I'll borrow it from this creep of a butler."

We both hung up then, and Lattimore was shaking his head again. "Why is it that when two Palm Beachers talk together they sound like gangsters?"

"Maybe it's the way the money was made," I told him.

"It's so direct, so wonderful," he said. "I'm just sorry you don't run the country."

"Palm Beachers run the country?" I couldn't believe my ears. "You must be out of your mind. They can't even run their own houses."

"A house is not a country," Lattimore said. "How come Brother Tifton was so ready to leave Chicago?"

"He didn't say, but I guess he was bored," I said. "He's always bored, though, always ready to get to the next place."

"That's the spirit that built the country," Lattimore said. "Daniel Boone, the wagon trains."

"It's just the old Palm Beach restlessness," I told him.

19

GRANMA GOT THERE FIRST, just before eight. She was in one of her jumpsuits and I thought Lattimore was going to fall over when he saw her.

She sat right down and pulled out five thousand in hundreds and spread them on the table and said, "There's the money, now give me the story." She pointed at Lattimore. "Is this the boy?"

We both laughed and said no, and then we told her everything. At the end she said, "I like it and I don't. I like the idea of getting that boy away from the Schreckers and stopping them, but I don't like the danger. You could get in a lot of trouble."

"We are already," I told her.

"And I don't like hiring a driver," she said. "It's a waste of money, too. I'll drive you."

"What if you get caught?"

"I'm an old woman. It won't matter so much."

Then we talked about the plan we had as she ate dinner. Lattimore couldn't take his eyes off her.

Dale pulled in about ten and came up. We had told Granma he was coming so she wasn't surprised. She knew him and didn't like him much, but she could see we needed him for the plan.

Dale is a terrible kid, but he never bores you and never wastes time. The ordinary kid would have come in with a lot of talk about how the airplane trip was and all that, but Dale just looked around the room and nodded his head at the three of us and said, "OK, fill me in."

I couldn't have told the whole story again, but with Dale we didn't have to. We just told him we were going to grab a kid at Camp Downing and take him over to Taddington.

"That's kidnapping," he said.

"More of a joke," I said.

"How come you need me? What are the problems?"

"This kid is tough. It's one of the Connollys."

"One of that bunch that comes to Palm Beach?"

"Uh-huh."

I thought that might put him off, but it didn't. "I don't like them," he said. "I wouldn't mind working one over."

Lattimore and Granma were looking at him like he was Al Capone.

"No *unnecessary* rough stuff," I told him. "And Lattimore and I are giving the orders. You have to do it our way. Exactly. OK?"

As tough as Dale is, I can lick him because I'm so big. We've had three or four fights and I've always won. If it wasn't for that I never would have gotten him to Boston. Being licked is the only thing he respects.

"OK," he said. "When do I hear the plan?"

"Tomorrow. On the way up."

"When do I get paid?"

"When we're done."

"Half now and the rest when we're done."

"I've already given you a hundred."

"I had expenses on the way. I only have fifty left."

"You won't need any more before we leave here."

"What do you mean? I'm going out tonight."

I finally gave him another hundred and made him promise he'd be in by one o'clock. We got him a separate room under the name of Alden before he went out.

When we were ready to go to bed ourselves, I went into Granma's room to tell her good night, and she said, "You're doing a lot for this Campbell boy. Is he worth it?"

"He's not worth much of anything," I said. "I'm doing it because . . . well, those Schreckers are just too much. That may sound like a small reason, but it's the best one I have."

"It'll do," she said.

"Why are you going along?" I asked her.

217

"You remind me of . . . someone," she said. "Of your grandfather, when he was young. You're the only one in the family who does. Maybe he made the fortune so that . . . so that you could do something like this, stop people like that. Maybe that's what it means, but whether it does or not, that's why I'm helping you. Now get to bed."

"All right, Granma."

"Turn the light out when you go." She was already in bed.

"Yes, Granma."

I was just closing the door when she said, "Ox."

"Yes."

"Even if it doesn't work, you handled it well. The way you called me and got that awful Tifton boy here and sat on him. Your grandfather would have been proud of you. Don't forget that—even if it doesn't work. And if there's trouble, I'll back you up. And I'll make your father back you."

"Thank you, Granma."

Then I closed the door and went back in my room and started to go to sleep.

20

WE HAD A TERRIBLE TIME getting Dale up in the morning. When we finally shook him awake I asked him
what time he'd gotten in.

"Tell me the truth," I said. "If you don't, I can
find out from the night porter."

"Before four," he said. "I've always heard Boston
was slow, but it wasn't that way last night."

"You don't get paid unless you're in shape," I said.
"We won't even take you with us."

"What time do you want to leave?"

"Noon."

"Let me sleep until then and I'll be ready."

So I did. Lattimore and I went out and bought the
stuff we needed—rope and flashlights and masks and

everything else we could think of. Granma took the Mercedes to a garage and tuned it herself. The mechanics watched her like she was some heart-transplant genius.

Lattimore couldn't get over her car. "I never saw one like it," he said.

"And you never will," she said. "It's a special body. The engine is, too. It'll do over a hundred and eighty on a straightaway."

"I hope we don't have to go that fast," he said to me later.

"Even if we do, she's supposed to know how to handle it," I said. "She's done a lot of racing."

We got Dale up at noon on schedule and he was in better shape. Then we ate, so we didn't get away until a little after one. But in that car it didn't matter. We were in Dexter by four thirty, and Granma hadn't been pushing it.

"We don't want to go into Dexter," I said. "Someone from the camp might see us. Let's go to a motel on this side of town."

She picked one out and we took two rooms under fake names that Lattimore thought up.

Then I explained the first part of the plan. Lattimore and I couldn't show up anywhere around Dexter or the camp. But no one in either place had ever seen Granma or Dale, so they could go anywhere.

They'd drive to the camp first and she'd pretend she was interested in putting her grandson in it for the rest of the season, or for the next year. While they were there, they were supposed to talk about all the recent excitement and get any information they could. Then they'd go back to Dexter and talk to people there and pick up what else they could.

Granma didn't much like the idea of even pretending Dale was her grandson, but she saw she had to. Dale didn't like it any better, just on principle, but he saw he had to, too. They were going to call themselves Standish, another one of Lattimore's inventions. "They make a wonderful pair," he said as they drove off. "And the name suits them."

I had a snack at the motel restaurant, and then we lay around and waited for them.

They came back about seven-thirty, and we all had dinner and they told us about their trip.

"That Skipper certainly is a marshmallow," Granma said. She seemed nervous. "I've never seen one like that. Anyhow, we got in to see him and signed Master Joshua Standish up for next year—the Skipper and his instructors know so many of Joshua's relatives and were a little surprised to find that Joshua seemed never to have heard of any of them. Finally we got past that and told the Skipper we'd heard Camp Downing had lost some horses recently, and that started him.

"They suspect you two, but they aren't sure. They got almost all the horses back, and the camp is supposed to be much calmer, but he says it will never be the same. 'I trust boys and I expect them to trust me,' he told us, almost with tears in his eyes. 'But never in my thirty years of working with boys have I been treated like that.' Then he started babbling about how he would have been willing to talk over using horse —'negotiate meaningfully' was the way he put it—and that there was no need to steal all the horses, or push horses. It didn't make any sense. Same thing about the postcards to the Schreckers. He almost passes out when he thinks of those. Not much of anything in Dexter. They talk about the great horse raid, but they don't know anything specific."

Granma had been talking too fast, for her, and then she stopped. She didn't look happy.

"Well, tell them," Dale said to her.

"I have bad news," she said.

"Let's have it," I said.

"Ox, the Connollys aren't there."

I could hardly take it in. "Where are they?"

"They've gone to some Connolly family regatta on the coast."

"When will they be back?"

"The Skipper didn't know. They might not come back this summer at all."

Lattimore and I just looked at each other. "We'd never get one out of the family corral," he said, sort of reading my mind. "They have that place patrolled like the White House."

"Who told you?" Lattimore asked Dale. "The Skipper?"

"I wasn't there," Dale said. "She told me on the way back."

"After a boy is enrolled, the Skipper likes to have

a private chat with the guardian," Granma said. "So Dale waited outside. It was then that I mentioned the Connollys casually—I think I said I'd heard they were there and such nice boys—and he told me. Now listen, Ox, I know what a disappointment this is, but it's not the end. Driving back out here I figured out another plan."

"We've had so many," Lattimore said.

"I think this one will work," Granma said.

"Want to tell us about it?" Lattimore asked her.

"Not yet," Granma said. "You and Ox kept your plan to yourselves and I'm going to do the same thing. All any of you need to know is that we're going to Taddington."

"But . . ." Lattimore began.

"No buts. I did your plan your way, and it's only fair that you do mine my way. All right?"

"All right," Lattimore said, and Dale and I agreed.

We packed up and piled into the car and started. Just to kill time—and to keep our minds off Granma's plan—Lattimore and I told them what our plan had been. We'd written it down in notes and Lattimore read it with a pencil flashlight. I still have the notes.

9:30—drive to back of camp, park on road ½ mile away. Granma stays with car, 3 of us go thru woods, come out by Connolly cabin. Dale pounds on door, yells something like "Come on out if you're not chicken." Lattimore and Ox hiding in bushes. When Cs come out and start pounding

Dale, we grab a C from behind, one the others aren't looking at. We have rope and tie him up. Also tape mouth and eyes. Take earmuffs to put on him so he can't hear us when we talk. Also masks for disguise. Not needed for Dale, though, because they've never seen him. Maybe in Palm B. in a crowd, but they won't remember that.

L and Ox carry tied-up, taped-up, ear-muffed-up C thru woods to car. Wait for Dale.

(We didn't mention that when the Connollys came swarming out they'd have made more than a fuss. They probably would have given Dale a lot of punishment. They wouldn't have held him, but they would have worked him over. Dale might have been in bad shape, but he would have made it back to the car. We were sure of that.)

Then to Pilgrim's Knob. To get past dogs, use pencil-sized repellers that shoot some kind of gas, the kind that people get for protection against muggers. When dogs are knocked out, roll them up in big net carried for purpose. Then bring the C in and up hill to chapel. Best place to leave him. House no good because can't hide him there even if possible to get in and out without being seen. Grounds no good because it's cruel to leave even a C on cold ground. Chapel good—door never locked because always open to anyone of any color, race or creed—Dacoolah told us Dr. S. always says that.

Most unlikely anyone will go in there after ten

at night, so good. Leave the C under bench there, wrapped in blanket. He'll be out by 8 in morning at latest, so won't even miss a meal. 1 uncomfortable night, not much to pay for important part he's going to play.

We leave then, and dump dogs out of net on way. They'll be up and around in ½ hour. No one will be able to figure out how anyone except Schreckers could have gotten past them. Then back into car and up to Dacoolah's, with quick stop at public phone to call Skipper at personal number at Downing. When he answers we turn on portable tape recorder and play him tape Ox made through blanket. Impossible to tell who it is, and sounds more like man than boy. Says, "This is Dr. Schrecker, in Taddington. 1 have Connolly boy and I'm going to keep him."

Then, hopefully, Skipper goes mad, Connollys go mad, all rush to Taddington. Along with FBI, local cops and Connolly security guards. We hide at Dacoolah's until fireworks start. They bust into Pilgrim's Knob and probably the whole town with them. The Schreckers deny having a C on the place, but the cops search and finally find him. Can't figure it out from there, but big trouble for the Schreckers. Big enough so their whole act falls apart and Tommy gets free.

"Not a bad plan," Granma said when Lattimore was through.

"It might even have worked," I said.

"Yes, isn't it nice to think so," Lattimore said sort

of bitterly, and no one else said anything until we were almost in Taddington.

Granma turned to me. "Now tell me how we get to the Schreckers."

"You don't want to go there," I told her. "They're crazy, they won't let you in, they . . ."

"I can take care of myself," Granma said. "Just tell me the way."

"I don't know, Mrs. Olmstead," Lattimore said. "It's pretty late and . . ."

"It's only nine forty-five," Granma said. "Now are you going to tell me the way or I do I have to ask in some gas station?"

There was no arguing with her, so we told her.

As soon as we got to the gates at Pilgrim's Knob, you could tell there was something wrong. They were wide open and sort of swinging on the hinges. When you looked up the drive, there was something different in the skyline, even at night. And there was a funny smell in the air.

It didn't take long before we were up the drive and the headlights swung around the last curve to where the house had been. Now there wasn't any house. It was leveled right to the ground, just like one of those houses in a city that's been bombed. There was wood and glass and junk spread all over the place, but nothing was left standing. There was still smoke rising from the wreckage. That was the funny smell.

None of us knew what to say. Or do.

Then I noticed something under the trees about a

hundred feet away, on the far side of the driveway circle. It was only a dim outline, but it looked familiar. I asked Granma to swing the car so the lights could pick it up. It was Doug, the old Model T pickup. It looked little and lonely, almost like it understood it was abandoned. As soon as I saw it I knew Dacoolah had had something to do with what we'd seen. And that we had to find out what had happened—and why—before we could think of Campbell. We were all worried sick about him, but we couldn't go off half-cocked.

21

OF COURSE, IT TOOK A WHILE to put everything together.
We went back to Dacoolah's and found her letter
and then we went to the police and found out what
they knew, and later we talked with people who had
seen it—or at least part of it. And still later we read
what the people who were there had said to reporters.
It was only then that we could try to put it together,
and even so we weren't sure it was right.

This is about as close as we could figure it.

After Dacoolah dropped us in Mallaby she drove
back to the quarry and stayed there for the rest of
that day, which was a Thursday, and all of Friday, and
Saturday until around noon. At least no one saw her
outside the quarry in all that time. That was about
two full days and she must have been thinking and

boiling away inside and getting ready. On Friday, while Lattimore and I were running around Boston seeing Mr. Lewis and Dr. Foster, she must have been sitting there in that old house driving herself wilder and wilder about the Schreckers.

On Saturday morning, while we were getting ready to go to Downing, she probably sat down to write her letter. It was to Lattimore and me, and when she was done with it she put it in the old refrigerator. That was how the police missed it when they went over the house later on Saturday. I found it Saturday night, after we left Pilgrim's Knob and drove to Dacoolah's. We went straight there. I was afraid we wouldn't find her when I saw Doug at the Schreckers because I couldn't imagine she'd leave her little truck there, but I was hoping.

The house was dark but the front door was un-locked and we went right in. We turned on some lights and I called "Dacoolah!" a few times. But there was no answer, just like I was afraid there wouldn't be.

There was the same old mess everywhere and we were all wandering around and I ended up in the kitchen, as usual. When I'm worried I get even hun-grier than usual, and so I opened the refrigerator door. I didn't expect much because it was Dacoolah's refrigerator, but it was force of habit and I figured that even hers couldn't be completely empty.

As soon as I opened the door I saw the envelope, propped up against one of the mustard jars. On the front it said, "For Ox and Lattimore."

Lattimore was in the dining room and I got him

229

and we went back to the kitchen and spread it out on the table and read it. Granma and Dale came in while we were reading, and after we finished they read it, too. Later the police and a lot of other people read it or heard about it and within a week it was in the newspapers, so it's no secret. She never meant it to be, either, or Lattimore and I wouldn't have handed it over. She wanted it to get around—she said so right in it. I guess she knew they'd call her crazy, so she tried to explain herself. But I think her other reason for writing it was to explain to Lattimore and me— and other kids, I guess—why she was going to do what she did, and I suppose it does some good that way. To a kid, I think it's pretty clear. I guess kids don't care so much whether other people are crazy or not as long as they're kind instead of mean.

Anyhow, here's what she said:

Dear Boys,

I am depending on Ox's stomach to get him to the refrigerator and this letter in case I don't come back this afternoon, and I really don't think I will be back. If I leave the letter out on a table, the police will get it first, and they may never show it to you. I don't mind them seeing it—after you read it you should let them if they wish—but I want you to read it first. Just make sure you get it back after other people do read it.

Since you left I've done a lot of thinking about you and Tommy and the Schreckers. I want you to know I've thought about you more than about the Schreckers. It's your positive qualities rather than their negative ones that are going to make me do what I'm going to do. I hope you will understand that. It's not that I care if they're winners, but that I won't let you be losers. If you were worthless, I wouldn't care. It isn't hate that's most important.

You aren't old enough to remember what the Nazis did, but perhaps you have heard people say they wouldn't have gotten very far if the decent Germans had stood up to them in the beginning. People think it would have been so easy for decent Germans to do that, but it never is easy to go against a government that seems to be in legal power. Americans who thought the saturation bombing of North Viet Nam was immoral have found that out, too.

In the past few days one thing has been going through my mind over and over. The Schreckers are like Nazis, though on a smaller scale (not as much smaller as you might think, however!) and a lot of decent people know that but no one will do anything about it. Am I supposed to be like every other adult and do nothing? Or am I supposed to be different and do what everyone really knows should be done?

I am only an old actress, I tell myself, so why should I have to do what no one else will do?

I try to get out of it like that, but I can't. Perhaps

other people can live with themselves after they
come to the great moral crisis of their lives and
fail it, but I can't. So I have to do something. I have
seen what this criminally insane pair do to
children—and adults—and now I must do something to stop them.

What will that be? Well, I shall go to them and
tell them they must let the boy go. If they refuse,
then I must do away with them. I know that
sounds awful, but what else is there? People say
that you shouldn't take the law into your own
hands, but what do you do when there is no law?

Many years ago, John Brown led an illegal raid
at Harpers Ferry—you know the story. He did it because someone had to stand up against slavery.
His action was illegal and he was killed, but do
we know that people would have been roused
to act legally (and why was the Civil War more
"legal" than what he did?) if he had not done what
he did? Isn't it strange that the Northern armies
marched to the music and words of *his* story—
"John Brown's body lies a-mould'ring in the grave"
—in preference to any other?

Well, when I start comparing myself to John
Brown, I know the old actress is taking over, and I
have to avoid that. But there has to be a certain
amount of drama in anything that's worth doing,
and who is better able to understand drama
than an old actress?

Why don't I have as much right as Churchill did
to put my cause in dramatic language and say

without shame that if I am playing my greatest role then I am doing no less than what he or Abraham Lincoln did? I only hope I can play it well and that it is a far, far better thing I do than anything I have done heretofore.

Good-bye, boys, and don't feel sorry for me or that you owe me anything. It truly is a far better thing I do, and really the only thing I can do.

Respectfully yours,
Dacoolah

When she finished that she went down to the sheds near the quarry and got the dynamite. It was left from when they'd used it years before to get the marble out. She knew it was there, and she knew it was still good, and she knew how to rig the bomb because she'd done a lot of that for her father in the quarry when she was young.

Then she put the bomb in her big handbag and drove over to Pilgrim's Knob in Doug. A maid opened the door and went to the library to tell the Schreckers Dacoolah was there to see them. They told her to show Dacoolah in.

A friend of theirs said afterward, "They knew Dacoolah. They even liked her because she was the village eccentric. They probably thought she was calling to talk about some local charity, and they were always great supporters of those. So naturally they let her in."

One of the maids was in the next room when Dacoolah was talking to the Schreckers, and she could hear everything. She said Dacoolah asked them to let Tommy go. They got excited and started yelling at her, and then she said, "All right, if that's the way you want it," and stood up and backed out of the room and locked the door behind her. Then she really had the Schreckers, because all the windows in the house were barred, and there was no way out for them. Dacoolah had been at Pilgrim's Knob often enough to know about the bars and the locks on the doors and all the rest. She had it all figured out.

"I knew something was wrong," the maid said later to the newspaper reporters, "but what could I do? She—Miss Tompkins—was standing over me with her eyes blazing like, and she opened that huge purse and took out that awful bomb and waved it at me. 'How many people are in the house?' 'Me and Josey and Tommy,' I told her. Josey's our cook. The other girl, Gladys, was off. 'Lord, have mercy on us, have mercy, Miss Tompkins!' and I went down on my knees. She jerked me up. 'Don't start that,' she said. 'I'm going to destroy this house, but I'm not going to hurt you. Or Josey or Tommy. You have five minutes to get yourself and them out—out on the lawn where I can see all three of you. Over where the lawn ends, by the trees. I don't want you too close.' What could I do? She was an actress, and she made it so real that I was up off my knees and running when she finished. People say I should have thought of the Schreckers, but those people weren't there. You could only think of that bomb."

So the maid got Tommy and the cook out on the

lawn, to the spot where Dacoolah had told them to go. The police asked them later why they didn't telephone to the station before they went out, and they said they knew the Schreckers had a telephone and an alarm system in the library, and could call the police themselves. But Granma said later, "Even their servants didn't care."

The Schreckers did make that call to the police while Dacoolah was talking to the maid, and the squad car got up there in ten minutes or so, but by then it was too late.

No one knows what happened inside at the end, but the maid and the cook and Tommy said it seemed they were standing on the lawn for a long, long time before the explosion came. My own guess is that when Dacoolah saw that Tommy and the two maids were safe, she unlocked the library door and went back in and showed the Schreckers the bomb and gave them one last chance. They refused and so she detonated it.

It went off a couple of minutes before the police got there—maybe she heard the sirens in the distance—and it was some explosion. People heard it miles away. There wasn't much left, and what there was went up in the fire.

Dacoolah probably could have left the bomb and run outside and saved herself, but that wasn't the way she had planned it—or what she wanted—so she perished with them.

22

OF COURSE, WE DIDN'T KNOW all that when we finished
reading Dacoolah's letter. All we knew was that something had happened and that we had to find out what.
And Campbell—I knew we had to get to Campbell.

We piled out of Dacoolah's poor old house, with all
the papers and mess looking so sad, and drove right
down to the Taddington police station. It was in a
Colonial building and there was a policeman in uni-
form behind the desk.

"I am Mrs. Franklin Olmstead," Granma said to
him. "I want to know what happened at the Schrecker
place today. In detail."

"That is police business," he said. "It is not . . . "

"I have material evidence," Granma said, waving

236

Dacoolah's letter at him. "You will tell me what happened."

He jumped up and tried to grab the letter, but Granma was too quick for him. And then Dale and I got between him and Granma, and we were both bigger than he was so he gave up.

"I'll call the Chief," he said, like he was threatening something, and he ran to a door in the rear of the room and disappeared through it.

"Let's get out of here," Dale said. "I don't want to go to jail."

"You will not move," Granma cracked out at him, and he didn't.

The policeman came back with the Chief, who was a big man with white hair and a calm manner.

"There they are!" the officer yelled. "They . . . "

"That's enough, Simmons," the Chief said. "Get back to the desk."

And Simmons did, although he was still glaring a little.

"I'm Chief Adams," the big man said to Granma. "Can I help you?" He didn't seem a bit upset by her jumpsuit or anything else.

Granma said afterward that as soon as he spoke to her she knew he was all right and everything was going to work out.

"I have a letter here that Miss Tompkins left for these boys, one of whom is my grandson. But I don't know what happened afterward . . . what she did. I want you to tell me."

"Could I see the letter?" the Chief asked her.

"After you tell me what happened," Granma said.

I thought that was the end of that, but he only sighed and said, "All right. Would you like to come into my office, where you can sit down?"

"Thank you," Granma said politely, and we all trooped in there and got chairs, and he told us everything he knew, all of which I've already explained.

"That's it," he finished. "Dacoolah went up there and blew herself and the Schreckers and the house to pieces. According to the maid, it was because they wouldn't let the boy go."

"I'll give you the letter to read now," Granma said. "And you can make as many copies as you wish. But you have to agree to give back this original. It belongs to these boys."

The Chief agreed and she handed it over. He read it carefully and then walked out and gave it to Simmons to make copies on a machine they had. When he came back in, he sat down and put his fingers together and looked at all of us.

"Well?" Granma asked him.

"Well, what?" the Chief asked back.

"Well, was she crazy or was she justified?"

"You know I have to say she was not justified," the Chief said. "What she did is never justified."

"What if the situation in this town was as bad as she says it was? As these boys here know it was—they roomed with Tommy Campbell at Camp Downing. As bad as I know it was—as it is, I should say."

The Chief didn't say anything for a while. By that time he must have known we were the ones from Downing who had caused all the trouble, but I guess he had bigger things on his mind than going after us.

"Suppose I surprised you, Mrs. Olmstead," he finally said. "Suppose I told you I knew it was bad. But there was nothing I could do because there were no legal grounds on which to proceed. As long as the boy himself didn't complain, what could anyone do?"

"If you told me that," Granma said, "I would still say that there must have been some way for the authorities in this town to have done *something*. But I won't press that point now. I will say, however, that we ought to make something constructive out of all this horror."

"How can we do that?" the Chief asked.

"If Tommy Campbell will tell the truth now, then what this Tompkins woman did will not have been done in vain. He told it all to these boys in private. Now he can tell it in public."

"He's at the Taddington Inn," Chief Adams told her. "And they're all there with him—the psychiatrist, the trust man from Boston, a bunch of local bigwigs, and then the relatives—Mrs. Warren, one of Mrs. Schrecker's daughters, and her husband, and I don't know who else. It won't be easy."

"You mean they'll try to keep us from him," Granma said.

"I'm sure they will."

"Then you'll have to get us in."

239

"On what grounds?" the Chief asked her.

"*On what grounds!*" Granma said, jumping up. "A woman killed herself and two other people here today —what more grounds can there be? Haven't you read that letter? Don't you understand plain English?"

The Chief was silent.

"You're right," he finally said. "I apologize. We've been told what to do and what to think for so long in this town that it's become a habit. But no more—I'll get you in there to that boy and I'll see that he has his chance to talk. The rest is up to him. And you."

The Taddington Inn is a big, fancy place about five miles outside the town. It's an old inn that was remodeled with all the comforts, and they say it's one of the best-known places in the East. We went out there behind the Chief, and he had his siren on and was going so fast that even Granma was working to keep up with him. He was really upset by then, and later that night we found out why.

We walked into the lobby of the Inn behind him. There was a policeman on duty and he came up to the Chief, and the Chief told him it was all right, and we went up to the suite where they all were.

On the way up, Granma asked the Chief why he had a man there.

"They wanted protection," he said, waving his hands sort of disgustedly. "They thought there might be . . . accomplices."

Granma smiled and he looked embarrassed.

When we got upstairs, the Chief knocked on the

door of the suite. The door opened and it was like looking at a painting. The door framed it and it was all balanced out, starting with the couch that you saw in the exact middle. And in the middle of the couch was Campbell, sitting there with Dr. Foster holding his hand on one side and Mr. Lewis on the other, and Judge Stella Smith and a few local lawyers hanging over the back. Behind them were groups of relatives and friends, all there for money reasons of one kind or another. They all stopped talking when the door opened and looked at us like deer when they sense trouble. They were frozen, and that was what made it look like a painting. Campbell looked scared, as usual, and acted like he hardly knew us.

The first person to move was the woman who had opened the door. She came out from behind it and said, "I am Mrs. Deering Gardner." She was tall and had on a long dress that was sort of purple and had a white collar. It looked old-fashioned. She had other old-fashioned things about her, too, like her hair in a bun, and a big floppy hat on, and walking shoes.

Granma opened her mouth to say something to Mrs. Gardner, but she never made it, because Mr. Lewis saw Lattimore and me and started screaming, "Get them out! Out! Out!"

"You calm down," Chief Adams said to him, and he did. "These people have important evidence in the case," the Chief went on, "and they're here on my orders and they're going to talk to young Tommy."

"You're exceeding your authority, Charley," Judge

Stella Smith said to him. She really did look tough, and she had a very deep voice and threw herself around like a sheriff in the Old West. You didn't have to be told who she was—you knew right away.

"I'll risk that," the Chief said.

"This may cost you your job," she said. She acted like she was going to pull a gun.

"That's part of the risk, isn't it?" he asked her. "All right," he said to our side, "go ahead and say what you want to Tommy."

"Not with all these people here," Granma said.

"We're not people," Mrs. Gardner said. "We're friends of the Schreckers." She had a very soft voice and when she talked she bent forward a little, because she was so tall. She looked something like pictures I've seen of President Roosevelt's wife, tall and not very pretty, but with a soft voice and nice to everyone. She was so gentle that anything she said seemed very reasonable, even when it wasn't.

"We are staying right here," some woman said to Granma. She turned out to be Mrs. Warren, Frances Warren, the daughter of Mrs. Schrecker's that Campbell had told us about. The one they kicked around over money, along with her husband, Paul. You'd have thought she'd been stepped on so much that she'd have been on our side, but she wasn't. At least not in the beginning.

So Lattimore and I talked to Campbell and reminded him of everything he had told us about the Schreckers and said that now was the time to tell the Chief and everyone else the truth.

He opened his mouth to do it, but then Mr. Lewis and Judge Stella Smith jumped on him and told him the Schreckers were saints and couldn't have done anything bad and that Lattimore and I were terrible troublemakers, and he closed his mouth.

While we had been talking to Campbell, the rest of the crowd had been listening to the stuff against the Schreckers like we were Charles Manson trying to lead a nice kid into a life of crime. They couldn't believe it was Campbell who had told us those things in the first place.

"Who are those boys?" Mrs. Gardner asked Granma in her soft way. She and Granma standing next to each other looked like people from different planets.

"The big one is my grandson," Granma said. "The other one is a boy named Lattimore." She didn't have to explain Dale because he hadn't been talking.

"The Schreckers were wonderful people," Mrs. Gardner said with a sigh. "They were relatives of mine. She was, anyhow—my sister. They were wonderful because they were so unhappy and so brave about it. She only married him because she thought he was dying, and after he was dead she could be a gracious widow and dispense good works. It was an attractive and worthwhile dream . . . and then it came to naught, because he kept disappointing her, year after year."

Granma sort of stared at her, as though she couldn't believe what she was hearing. So did we. You might think Mrs. Gardner was being sarcastic, but she was so gentle and spoke so sincerely that you knew she couldn't be.

Lattimore was behind her and he rolled his eyes at me to show that he thought she wasn't all there. I was already thinking that myself, but I wasn't sure. People like that can be more there than anyone else. When you looked into Mrs. Gardner's eyes, you could tell they were seeing something faraway and long ago, but as Dad says, when you get far enough away and long enough ago, you start coming back the other way and you end up closer in and ahead of the rest of us.

Anyhow, with Mrs. Gardner it was hard to tell which she was.

"May I talk to you, Tommy?" Granma asked Campbell.

"No!" Mr. Lewis said.

"Why not?" a little bald-headed man asked him. "Talk is cheap. Especially at a wake like this."

Granma was already talking to Campbell, and the little bald-headed man said to me, "Everyone in Boston loved the Schreckers. They knew all the best people— if you believe in best people, and we have to, even when we don't. They were so lovable, how could the best people resist them? No best people, have to invent them. Voltaire said that. No? Then he should have. Anyhow, if the Schreckers were good enough for the best, how could they have been so bad? You tell me. Can you?"

I told him I couldn't.

"Pity," he said. "Do you know Frankie Fitzgerald?"

I told him I didn't.

"Smart girl," he said. "Smartest girl in Boston. She

244

can explain it all to you. My name is Hackett. My friends call me Hurry-Up."

I couldn't make head or tail out of what he was saying, and anyhow I was trying to listen to Granma. She was telling Campbell that Lattimore and I were his friends and had done so much for him and that all he had to do was stand up for once and tell the truth. Lattimore said later that she gave him a wonderful speech, but I didn't hear a quarter of it because Hurry-Up Hackett was glued to me and telling me all about how he used to wear dancing pumps to play touch football when he was at Harvard. He was about sixty and didn't look like he'd ever had any exercise. But he was still wearing dancing pumps, along with an old tweed suit.

When Granma was through with him, Campbell was all ready to tell the truth, but then Mrs. Warren sat down next to him and put her arms around him and begged him not to say anything against the Schreckers he'd regret because they were such great people. "I beg you," she kept saying. "You are tired now, and perhaps you don't know what you mean. You have to remember that Granny and Grampy are beacons, showing you the way. Always." She went on and on like that, talking like they were still alive.

Then Lattimore and I had another crack at Campbell. While we were talking to him, Mrs. Gardner and Hurry-Up Hackett were right behind us having a conversation about the Schreckers.

"She was my sister," Mrs. Gardner said to him. "She

245

was a beast, I suppose, but she was my sister."

"She was Life," Hurry-Up said. "She was the great Earth-Mother. She nursed half New England."

"She was my sister," Mrs. Gardner said. "Blood can be so important, but it's probably overrated."

There was so much noise in the room I could hardly think, but I kept going. So did Lattimore. When we finally ran down, the other side moved in again. It was like a tug-of-war, with Campbell in the middle. Back and forth it went.

The room was full of smoke, and a lot of them were drinking, and it was getting hotter. But most of all it was the noise from everyone talking at once that drove me crazy. In one corner of the room, Mrs. Warren's husband, Paul, was making a speech to the Chief about how the Schreckers were dead and it was a sacrilege to talk about them, and besides they were from Taddington, and the Chief was shirking his duty by taking the side of outsiders, meaning us. In another corner, Judge Stella Smith was saying to Granma, "You try it! You just try it! You try it and I'll lock you up for criminal conspiracy!" Granma was laughing at her. Somewhere else I could hear Mrs. Gardner telling Mr. Lewis about how she wondered who she was and why she was who she was. Hurry-Up Hackett was telling Dr. Foster, "I accept you because you're a Boston psychiatrist. You're Boston before you're psychiatric. That's why you're acceptable. Think it over." Then Dr. Foster tried to explain to him that it didn't make any difference where a psychiatrist came from, but Hurry-Up wasn't having any of that. Mrs. Warren was holding Campbell's hand and crying. It was supposed to be her turn at him, but she wasn't using it except to cry. Campbell was staring straight ahead. Some people near the door were arguing about when the first symphony concert would be in Boston that fall. A man was down on all fours looking for his wife's earrings and she was yelling at him. Another man was drinking toasts to the Schreckers all by himself, at the table where they had the liquor. An old man with white hair was telling his wife that he could stand anything except excess. And . . . but I couldn't begin to describe all of it.

"New England on the half-shell," Lattimore said to me. "Too bad we can't preserve it on film."

I've listened to the noise from a lot of Palm Beach parties, but that noise always seems to be on one level, the fun level, with everyone trying to have a better time than everyone else. But this noise was on different levels, I guess because they were all pulling in different directions. Anyhow, it had me spinning, and I decided it would be better to listen to one conversation and try to blot out the others. So I went over to the corner where Mrs. Warren's husband was telling the Chief how he shouldn't be taking the side of outsiders.

The Chief listened to all that and said, "You seem to forget that the Schreckers were not from Taddington originally. Dacoolah was, and she's as dead as they are, and I intend to find out why."

I knew then why he'd been sore, driving out. Someone from a real Taddington family, an old one, had been forced to do something terrible, and that finally got to him. He couldn't stand it. After all, he and Dacoolah were about the same age. Maybe they'd gone to school together. Maybe he liked her a lot, when they were kids. They say those things can come back to you.

Next to me, a woman was laughing behind her hand at Granma's jumpsuit and I said to her, "That's some outfit, isn't it."

"I never saw anything like it," she said. "But aren't you with her?"

"She's my grandmother."

"Well, I didn't mean to be rude, but you people have no business here." She went on talking like that and finally told me she was Campbell's other aunt, the one named Peggy. Her full name was Mrs. Davis Calhoun.

While I was listening to her, Granma came over and I said, "This is Mrs. Calhoun, and she thinks your jumpsuit is a howl."

"I saw her laughing at it," Granma said.

Mrs. Calhoun got red and said, "You don't seem to understand that Pilgrim's Knob and the people in it are gone. Don't you have any respect for the dead?"

Granma said to me, "Ox, correct me if I'm wrong, but I'm under the impression that none of these people have any respect for anyone, dead or alive. Is that right?"

"That's right, Granma," I said. "All they care about is trust funds."

"If they think of nothing but money, and other people's money at that, then they must be poor people. Am I correct?"

"They're church mice, Granma."

"You can't talk to me that way," Mrs. Calhoun said.

"I wasn't aware that I was talking to you," Granma said, "but I will now." She had raised her voice just a little and almost everyone in the room stopped to listen. "No, I don't have any respect for the Schreckers and I'll tell you why. When I saw Pilgrim's Knob tonight I felt like my old friend Harry Truman did when he saw Berlin in 1945. He said then, 'Well, I guess they had it coming.' That's what I say about the Schreckers. I guess they had it coming."

That touched off some real excitement. The whole mob crowded around Granma and started screaming. Except Mrs. Gardner and Mrs. Warren. Mrs. Gardner had her arms around Mrs. Warren, who was crying and saying, "They weren't nice people, but no one should talk about them that way."

"No, no one should," Mrs. Gardner said in her soft, vague way. "But the Germans *did* have it coming, and . . . who knows?"

"Aunt Rebecca!" Mrs. Warren cried out, leaning back. "You can't mean that the Schreckers were that bad!"

"She was my sister," Mrs. Gardner said. "But I can't pretend I liked her after she grew up. It was lovely when we were children, especially in the summers. We went to Europe, you know, to a villa Daddy had in

249

Dubrovnik. Everyone else went to the Cape or Maine, but we went to Dubrovnik. We were lucky . . . and we were all friends then. But afterward . . . no, she changed. And he was always awful."

"I can't stand it!" Mrs. Warren sobbed.

"They were awful to you, my child," Mrs. Gardner said.

"I can't stand it," Mrs. Warren moaned again. "You're mad. You can't help it, but you are." She broke down then and the tears were really pouring out. Mrs. Gardner had one arm around her and was patting her head absentmindedly with her free hand. She caught my eye and smiled in a gentle way.

"It was so lovely on the Adriatic then," she said. "It was long before Tito. Is that his name? They say Communism spoils all the fun. I daresay they're right."

Mrs. Warren had stopped crying and was wiping her eyes when Granma finally got away from the mob and came over to me.

"Let's go," she said. "This wretched boy isn't worth saving. And we've done everything we can."

"Wait a minute," I said. "He may not be worth saving, but Dacoolah is."

"That woman!" Hurry-Up hissed. "That Down-East murderess!"

"A lunatic," Mr. Lewis said. You could tell he meant that she wasn't even good enough to be a murderess. She was only crazy.

"You're right," Mrs. Warren said to him.

"She did a terrible thing," I told Mrs. Warren. "No

one can say she didn't, and I'm not trying to. But she wasn't a lunatic. She was completely sane."

"I will not be lectured to by this overgrown *brat*," Mr. Lewis shouted. "I . . . "

"Just let me say my little piece about Dacoolah," I said to Chief Adams. "Then I'll go. We'll all go. It'll only take a few minutes, and I owe it to her."

"All right," the Chief said. "Now just relax, Mr. Lewis. As the boy says, it will only take a few more minutes."

They all quieted down, and I pulled Dacoolah's letter out. "This is what she wrote before she did it," I said, "and I want you all to hear it."

I read it straight through, trying to keep my voice steady. I did, too, except at the very end, where I got a little wobbly.

I didn't look up once while I was reading, but I did when I finished and everyone on the other side looked sort of stunned and no one was saying anything. That letter packs a wallop.

"Well, that's it," I said, putting it in my pocket. "She was wrong, but she wasn't crazy. She was a decent old woman who'd been pushed too far. If any of the rest of you had drawn the line a long time ago she wouldn't have had to do what she did. You're to blame for what happened, not her. All right, let's go," I said to Granma.

"Wait," Mrs. Warren said. "You can't go now."

We all stood where we were and then she went over to Campbell.

"That letter, Tommy . . . " she said to him. "When I was listening to it, I felt as though I was waking from a dream. They *were* tyrants, they did do terrible things . . . to all of us. Especially to you, but to Paul and me, too, and to everyone they came in contact with. It's time we faced that, Tommy, it's time we admitted it."

"You leave him alone," Mr. Lewis said to her. "You . . . "

"You leave her alone," Dale said. It was something for him to say that, because he never stands up for a girl or a woman of any kind. But he did then, and when Dale puts that snarl into his voice he can scare you. He scared Mr. Lewis, and even Chief Adams looked like he was seeing a really dangerous gangster or something. Dale has that pure underworld quality.

Whatever it was, it shut Mr. Lewis up, and maybe Dale is the only one who could have done that.

"Come on, Tommy," Mrs. Warren said in a sort of tired, sad way. "Let's be honest."

"They say it's the best policy," Mrs. Gardner said very gently. "They truly do."

Campbell looked around and opened his mouth and this time no one was stopping him and he kept going. He told the whole story of how they had worked on him and he put in details he hadn't even told us. Every so often he'd cry a little, but then he'd pull himself together and keep going.

When he was finished there wasn't a sound from anyone.

252

Chief Adams gave them plenty of time and then he said to Mr. Lewis, "Well, do you have anything to say to that testimony?"

"We aren't in a court of law," Mr. Lewis said. "We . . ."

"We have a record, in case we do get that far," the Chief said. "Officer Grinnell has been in the other room taping all this. I hope Tommy will be able to repeat his testimony at the coroner's inquest. But if he isn't, we will use this."

"You had no right to do that," Mr. Lewis said. "You . . ."

"Oh, come off it, Hugo," Dr. Foster said. "They say it takes a big man to admit a mistake," he said to Lattimore and me. "I don't think that's true, because I feel very small, but I want to say I was wrong. You were right."

That was the end of the fight. Once Campbell told the truth they all had to cave in. The ones who were a little more decent or smarter, like Mrs. Warren and Dr. Foster, did it the fastest. It took the dumb ones, and the greedy ones who had been getting the most out of it, like Mr. Lewis and Judge Stella Smith, the longest. But in the end they all had to admit that Campbell was telling the truth and that the Schreckers had been monsters.

The only ones who didn't have to do any admitting were Mrs. Gardner and Hurry-Up Hackett, because they were so far out that they hadn't been all that involved in the first place. They didn't even seem to know it was all over, because Hurry-Up was telling Lattimore that he should go to Harvard, as though that was the most important thing in the world.

"But I don't want to go to Harvard," Lattimore told him. "I want to go to Michigan State."

"What do you want to do a crazy thing like that for?" Hurry-Up asked him.

"I want to get out there where people are people," Lattimore said. "Decency and football teams and cheerleaders and fresh apple pie. It's too decadent here in the East." Lattimore liked to tease people, especially people like Hurry-Up, and he knew how to do it.

Mrs. Gardner was talking to Granma about Harry Truman. "My husband knew him well," she said. "From Potsdam on. They all said he was honest enough, but terribly ambitious."

"In what way?" Granma asked her.

"My dear, I never thought to ask," Mrs. Gardner said. "Wasn't that silly of me?"

And the rest of them . . . well, people can change so fast. In half an hour they were all jumping up and down and saying they'd known all along how bad it was. Dr. Foster said to me, "I had my suspicions, of course, but what could I do? I never had enough to go on."

That made me sort of sick, and I said, "You had more than Lattimore and I had, and we're only kids and you're supposed to be the psychiatrist. You were seeing Campbell for years, weren't you? And you knew the Schreckers for a long time. No, I can't buy that, Dr.

Foster. You were more honest a minute ago when you said you were just plain wrong. Now you're forgetting that you never did anything when you had the chance, and that you never would have done anything if that poor old woman hadn't killed herself to make you see the truth. She was right about all of you."

I wasn't talking loud, but they'd all stopped what they were saying and were listening. That sort of made me sick, too, and I was wondering why it had to be me talking. It should have been them saying those things. The way they could forget everything was worse than when they'd been our enemies, and it made me feel terrible.

"Let's go," I said to Granma and the rest of our bunch. And that time we did go, Campbell included.

"Be careful on the road back to Boston," Hurry-Up called after us.

"Perhaps they aren't going that way," Mrs. Gardner said. "They might be going to some southern destination . . . Philadelphia, New York."

"Or even New Iberia, Louisiana," Lattimore called back.

"Dear me, yes," Mrs. Gardner said. "Down where the moss grows on the tree trunks—but I can never remember which side."

We marched down to the lobby and Granma said, "It just occurred to me—go where? If this place has any rooms we'd better stay here."

We'd all been so keyed up that no one had thought of that, and it was about two in the morning. So we got some rooms and stayed there. Before Chief Adams left he shook hands with all of us and said, "I hope I don't make the same mistake Dr. Foster did. I won't forget how this happened and why. And my own share in it. All I can say is that if anything like it comes up again I won't wait. That isn't much, though, and I know it."

Then we all went to our rooms and to bed. Usually I can go right off to sleep, but that night I tossed and turned. I kept seeing Dacoolah driving into Pilgrim's Knob in that funny little pickup, with her face set and ready to do what she had to do. "You were better than anyone," I said into the dark, as though she was there to hear it. I meant it, too.

23

LATTIMORE WOKE ME UP the next morning about ten and told me Anne and his mother had arrived. I got dressed and went down and had breakfast with Anne, and she told me how they'd gotten there.

"Mother said it was time we found out what my brother was doing," she said. "He called me yesterday from Boston and told us to come to Taddington today, that he hoped everything would be settled. So we started down and stayed the night a couple of hundred miles from here. And then got up at six this morning and drove the rest of the way."

"He took a chance telling you to come here and that everything would be settled. It got settled, but not the way we thought it would," I said.

"I know all about what happened, Ox. And I'm as sorry as you that it was settled the way it was. I know that was an awful price to pay—I'm not so dumb."

She wasn't, either.

The Taddington Inn was a fancy place and even the breakfast menu was in French. I asked Anne to translate.

"Can't you read *any* French?" she asked me.

"No. I can't speak it or understand it, either. Except for one sentence. There used to be a Frenchman in Palm Beach—he was looking for a rich widow—who always asked, *'Est-ce que votre piscine est chauffée?'* That means, 'Is your swimming pool heated?'"

"I know what it means," Anne said. "Even with your very original accent."

I didn't pay any attention to that. "It's the only French I know," I said, "and I wouldn't know even that much if he hadn't asked it so often. It was about all he ever said."

She shook her head just like Lattimore. "My brother's right," she said.

"Right about what?"

She wouldn't tell me.

But she did order for me, and I had three waffles with bacon and four fried eggs with ham and a sauce on top. It wasn't bad, but I still don't see why the menu had to be in French.

I was just finishing up when the Skipper and Peabody and Greening came marching into the dining room. They had Lattimore with them, too. I thought maybe they were going to arrest us or something, but Lattimore was grinning and I knew it was all right.

Lattimore sat down and the Skipper cleared his throat and started. "You two were the first to know," he said. "You were the first to point the finger at this terrible situation here in Taddington, at the Schreckers. And you put your beliefs on the line. You stole horse—I mean horses—and you caused untold grief with your postcards and . . . other activities. But you did it in a righteous cause! Will you accept my apologies? And those of every instructor at Camp Downing? We doubted, when we should have believed. We didn't have faith."

And Greening and Peabody said, "Hear, hear."

I was having a hard time keeping a straight face, and Anne was almost choking. She'd heard *about* them, but she'd never heard them in action.

Then the Skipper asked us about coming back to Downing. He acted like he was so much in the wrong that we'd be doing him a favor if we did.

"I'll come if I don't have to exercise," I said.

"Those are very hard terms, Ox," he said. "What will the other boys think?"

"That's their problem," I said, and he finally agreed. He told me later he thought I was going to ask to have my own pusher in the woods again, and he'd probably have had to let me. I was going to tell him then that I'd never had a pusher, but I winked instead. And he winked back.

Then we told him we wanted Campbell to come

back, too, and he said that it would be "beyond his fondest dreams" if Campbell would agree to come back, and we said we'd ask Campbell about it.

Dale came into the dining room and the Skipper stuck out his hand and said, "Hello, Standish," and Dale had to shake hands with him. The Skipper said he was looking forward to having him next year and asked what he was doing in Taddington, and a dozen other questions. We'd completely forgotten about Dale and Granma going to see the Skipper. And I never knew the Skipper had such a memory for names and faces.

Anyhow, Dale muttered something about looking forward to next summer, too. Then we all drifted away.

I paid Dale off in the men's room at the Taddington Inn. He wanted to get back to Boston in a hurry. We had a little argument as to whether he should get the rest of the five hundred, because we hadn't gone through with kidnapping the Connolly, but I finally gave it to him because we'd straightened everything out anyhow, and he'd stayed with us all the way. And put the evil eye on Mr. Lewis at the crucial moment.

"You could go down to Boston with Granma," I told him when we were finished.

"She has to drop you first and fool around," he said. "I've got another ride." He wouldn't tell me who it was, or what he was up to in Boston.

"I'll see you in Palm Beach," I said.

"You do that," he said, which was a pretty friendly

remark from Dale. He usually said something like, "Not if I see you first."

Then Lattimore and I talked to Campbell about going back to Downing, and he said he'd like to. He was almost normal again, for him. His aunt, Mrs. Warren, said she was happy he was going back. And happy that he had such good friends. We didn't see any of the rest of the old Schrecker gang.

So that was that, and Granma drove us all over to Downing—Lattimore and Campbell and me and Anne and Mrs. Lattimore. Granma and Mrs. Lattimore got on pretty well, and when Granma asked her to come with us she said she'd love to.

"I've never had a chance to ride in a car like this," she said, "and I'm not going to miss it."

Granma said she'd bring them back to Taddington and their own car later.

Even with the car's special body, it was kind of a tight squeeze in the car, but we were all friends, even Campbell, so we didn't notice it. There was a feeling of sadness, of course, but we started talking and Lattimore was pretty funny about Dale, and Granma told about her racing days and the rest of us threw in something every once in a while, so we all had a pretty good time.

After the others got out of the car at Downing, Granma asked Lattimore and me to stay and then she said, "When I told you that night that the Connollys weren't here at Downing I wasn't telling the truth. They were here, but I couldn't let you commit a kid-

261

napping. Besides, I don't think it would have worked."

Lattimore and I were so surprised we just sat there, and then I said, "You could have stopped us in Boston —you didn't have to wait until we were up here."

"No, I couldn't, because I didn't know how, without making you angry. And I didn't want to do that, because then we would have had a fight and wouldn't have stuck together to do something else."

"What was the something else?" I asked her. "What was the plan you said you had?"

"It wasn't really a plan," she said. "It came from my having lied to you. I was so ashamed of lying—it was so out of character for me—that I couldn't do it unless I assumed the responsibility for doing the very thing that I had to keep you from doing at such danger to yourselves. Can you follow that? Anyhow, I was just going to march into that Schrecker house and start. If they'd thrown me out I would have stayed in Taddington until I could bring public opinion around, no matter how long it took. Sometimes money is a great help. I would have done everything and anything. It even occurred to me that I might buy a newspaper and go after them. In the end I would have exposed them. We would have won."

"Don't feel bad about stopping us, Mrs. Olmstead," Lattimore told her. "If you hadn't, we would have shown up in Taddington that night with the Connolly, and would have found . . . well, what we did find. It was bad enough without having the Connolly on our hands."

He was right, and I told her so, too.

"It's nice of you to say that, both of you, but I didn't know I was right at the time. I was only some-one telling a lie then, and very miserable about it." She pushed her goggles around and got out of the car. "I know we can't forget what happened—ever," she said. "But let's not dwell on it, either."

That was the way we felt, so we went into the main lodge and sat around and had as good a time as we could until it was time for them to go.

It was like that for the rest of the summer. The camp was so organized that there was nothing to it. The Skipper always fell all over us, and so did the instructors. Even Swanson behaved himself. Even the Connollys came down to our cabin and lined up and told us they admired us for spotting the Schreckers. From the Connollys that was a lot. We were afraid they'd want us to be friends and fool around with them, but they didn't. After they made that speech we never had any more to do with them. I think their guards made them do it, for their image.

"You sure have this place organized," Russell said to me one day. "No exercise, lying around all the time. The Skipper practically waiting on you with his own hands. Swanson practically your servant."

"It's so good it's boring," I said. "It was more fun the other way."

"I know what you mean," he said. "When we used to tease Swanson and the others."

I finally got so bored I took up exercise again. That sounds impossible to believe, but it's true. I even started riding Klondike again. He'd been recaptured, and something must have happened to him the night we rode to Taddington because his shaking had really tapered off. Not completely, of course, but I could ride him in the normal way, and it wasn't bad at all.

Granma took a place over on the coast in New Hampshire for the rest of the summer, and she came to camp every so often and took us back there for the day. And Anne and Mrs. Lattimore came down from Maine a couple of times.

Everything got straightened out for Campbell. His aunt, Mrs. Warren, came to Downing a lot and showed that she understood what had happened and why. She didn't talk about it, but you could tell she did, so Campbell asked her if she'd be his guardian from then on. She said it would be an honor. Granma and Mrs. Lattimore have something to do with keeping an eye on the whole arrangement. And Campbell's money is being kept safe for him. His trust fund has been transfered to another bank Granma picked out because she's on the board there.

With everything straightened out, Campbell came back to life like a plant that's had some water poured on it.

"You saved my life," he told Lattimore and me. "I didn't have the guts to do it for myself, and I'll never forget it."

That was the only speech he made about it and I was glad it was a short one. It was good to see him normal. Normal for him, that is, because he'll probably always be a little jumpy and peculiar after what he's been through. That's why, when he said we'd saved his life, we didn't tell him it wasn't us but Dacoolah. Maybe he'll be able to face things like that someday, but not yet.

Dacoolah's name is cleared, in a way. She's still on record officially as a crazy murderess, but the people in Taddington know she thought she had a good motive. And they think so, too. "In five hundred years they'll probably put up a statue to her and carve her letter on the pedestal," Lattimore said. I told him I didn't think so, and he claimed that's the way all the saints, like Joan of Arc, got anointed. I still don't think so, because it's hard to imagine that Taddington will last that long, even if they're still making saints out of people.

I felt very bad about Dacoolah for a long time myself, but then I kept reading that letter of hers, and I decided that she really believed in what she did, so it wasn't sad after all.

It was almost at the end of the summer when Mrs. Warren was talking to Lattimore and me one evening in front of our cabin. Campbell was off doing something else. We were talking about nothing in particular, and then she said to me, "It's nice that you're so independent. I used to resent independence in people because I was too cowardly to get it for myself. Paul and I could have been independent and lived within our income and told my mother and Dr. Schrecker we didn't need their help. But we thought we had to have so many things . . . and then they had us. Anyhow, I don't resent independence in others any more. I wish them well. I wish you well."

I didn't know what to say to that except, "Thanks."

"If there is ever anything I can do for you two, let me know," she said.

"There is one thing," Lattimore said.

"What is it?"

"I'd certainly like to see Mrs. Gardner and Hurry-Up Hackett again," Lattimore said. He had a real appetite for people like that.

"You would? You mean because they're so odd?"

"They've got a lot of style," Lattimore said. "Especially Mrs. Gardner. You don't see style like that much any more."

"All right," Mrs. Warren said. "I'll bring them up here sometime, if they'll come."

It was the next to last day of camp when Mrs. Warren brought Mrs. Gardner and Hurry-Up Hackett. Lattimore and I were coming back from riding, and there were the three of them standing near the main building. Mrs. Gardner had on the same dress and still looked like a ship under full sail. Hurry-Up was uncomfortable and even shy. He and Mrs. Gardner didn't get in the sun much, I guess, because they were pale and their eyes were wrinkled up against the sun and they kept looking for shade, like moles that are always after cool dark places.

"What ho!" Hurry-Up said to us. "How do you stand the heat up here?"

"We had a perfect drive," Mrs. Gardner said. "New England is so lovely just now . . . golden leaves, pumpkins."

"Why, Aunt Rebecca, it's still high summer," Mrs. Warren said nervously. "The leaves haven't begun to turn, and pumpkins are months off."

"We can imagine, though," Mrs. Gardner said softly. "They say that's why God gave us our imaginations. Imagination distinguishes us from the beasts."

"That's right," Lattimore said. He was right in his element.

Then the Skipper came along and fell all over himself because Mrs. Gardner was such an important Bostonian.

And he and Hurry-Up were a pair. "Hardly Faneuil Hall," Hurry-Up said, pointing to the main lodge, "but I suppose it's comfortable enough."

"It's not supposed to be comfortable," the Skipper said coldly. "This is not a country club."

"Sure it is," Hurry-Up said. "The kids just haven't told you yet."

It took an effort, but the Skipper ignored that remark. Then he insisted on taking the whole party around the camp. When we got within sight of the Connolly cabin he explained about them and Mrs. Gardner said, "I think it's wonderful that you have a program for all kinds of boys, even the disadvantaged."

The Skipper's face was a study and Lattimore was in heaven.

Hurry-Up got me to one side and asked me if I knew where Dale was. I told him I didn't.

"I saw him . . . in Boston," he said. "Charming boy, but he seems to have . . . um . . . enormous financial problems. I loaned him a considerable sum and he said he'd send it back in a week. It's been several weeks now and I'm getting worried."

"Forget it," I said. "Dale never pays back."

"I'll sue him," Hurry-Up said. "Palm Beach hillbilly."

"How can you sue a kid?" I asked him. "People would only wonder why you were dumb enough to lend money to a minor."

He chewed on that a while and then said, "I guess you're right. Chalk it up to experience. You certainly don't learn about boys like Dale at St. Mark's."

"No," I said, "those hillbillies can fool you."

I was getting tired of all of them, so I dropped off.

Lattimore stayed for the whole tour, and it was almost dark when he came down to the cabin. "Wonderful," he said. "Wonderful woman. Completely batty, but wouldn't hurt a fly. Isn't it interesting that she and her sister were both bonkers, but it took them differently? One a killer whale and the other just a quiet old porpoise." He had theories on everything and some of them were pretty good.

When camp broke up, everyone fell all over everyone else and we all said we'd stay in touch. Russell gave me his address and I gave him mine, and I did the same thing with a lot of other kids. I must have had fifty addresses in the end. We all knew we weren't going to stay in touch, but you say so, anyhow.

Mrs. Lattimore and Anne came down to pick Lattimore up, and we all said good-bye.

"He's coming to Philadelphia at Christmas," Lattimore told them.

"He'd better," Anne said.

"If he doesn't, I'll go down and get him," Lattimore said.

"I'll go with you," Mrs. Lattimore said. She kissed me on the cheek. I'd gotten so tall I had to bend over so she could reach me. While I was leaning over like that she stepped back and Anne kissed me on the other cheek. "*Au revoir,*" she said.

I didn't get it and I must have looked kind of stupid, because she laughed and said, "That means good-bye."

"They never say good-bye in Palm Beach," Lattimore said. "Especially in French."

"What do they say?" Anne asked him.

"Something informal," he said. "Something like 'See you at the club.' Good-bye is too definite."

They were teasing me, but in a very special way. You could tell that by the way they smiled. They were the nicest people I'd ever met and I would have told them so except that you can't say things like that.

Then Granma said good-bye to them and it was time to leave. She was going to drive me to New York and I'd get a plane for Palm Beach there.

I tossed my stuff in the back of the Mercedes and climbed in beside her. She pulled her goggles down and revved the engine a couple of times and we took off.

I looked back and there were a lot of the boys waving. The Skipper and Peabody were still there, too. Lattimore was shaking his head.

Granma and I didn't talk much on the way down.

At the airport she had a beer and I had a meal while we waited for the plane.

"I guess we'll never forget this summer," she said. "I'm only thankful it turned out at all."

"As bad as it was, it could have been worse," I said.

"It could have been a lot worse," she said. "If it hadn't been for you, it would have been."

"For me? I didn't do any more than anyone else. I didn't do as much as you did."

"Yes, you did. You did a lot more than anyone. When you read that woman's letter up in that hotel room, you made it all . . . if you could have heard yourself . . . if you could have seen their faces . . ." She was looking down and a little away, so I couldn't see her face. "I can't say any more about it, Ox," she said. "Shouldn't give you ideas about . . . shouldn't make you grow up too soon, spoil your youth. There's time later—that's almost all there is later."

I knew what she meant and I didn't, right at the same moment. Then we talked about other things, ordinary things.

When it was time to go, she reached down in her pocket and pulled out a little box and handed it to me. "Open it on the plane," she said. She was acting kind of funny and I took her hand and asked her if she was all right.

"Sure I'm all right," she said, but then she put her

arms around me and laid her head against my chest. It was only for a second or two, but it wasn't like her. She felt like a child. Like the way she was when she was a girl, I thought.

Then she was walking away and people were staring at her jumpsuit and goggles.

I opened the box on the plane and inside was an old gold pocket watch. I fiddled with the cover on the back until it opened and inside it said, "To Franklin Spencer Olmstead from his loving wife, 1921." It was Granpa's watch and she'd given it to him then, when they had no money. It was as though she'd spent ten million today. I didn't think she should have given it to me, because it was probably the only heirloom in the whole family. And the only thing that had really cost anything.

24

CHARLES MET ME at the airport in West Palm Beach and was just the same. He made a few nasty remarks about how he didn't see why he had to drive over to get me, and I finally said, "You haven't had a thing to do all summer, have you? Everyone's been gone, and you've been loafing for two months, so why gripe about one trip to the airport?"

"I had plenty to do," he said. "The house is more work when it's closed than when it's open. You have to go in all the time to check the dehumidifiers. I had to give up one of my rooms over the garage to Rachel and it's not easy living cramped up." He went on and on like that.

Rachel had dinner ready and it wasn't very good. She even has trouble with a steak.

Dad was still on the safari. Mom was in Europe, but expected back in a few days. That was why the house was open again. If she hadn't been coming I guess I would have had to sleep with Charles over the garage.

It wasn't long before I was back in the old routine. There were still three weeks before school opened and I could do what I wanted again. Late sleeps, the Coral Beach for lunch, and to bed when I felt like it. I could eat what I pleased, too, and I started to get fat again. I didn't care. Like Dad says, pollution and the end of natural resources mean the end of everything, so why not be comfortable on the way out? I don't like to have that philosophy, but I always get it when I'm alone. Even though it sounds right, it doesn't make me feel any less lousy.

Mom wasn't home very long, just a few days to switch wardrobes and take off for San Francisco. I knew that when Dad got back he'd have a fit about the house being opened up just for her to do that, and I told her so.

"Let him," she said. "Just let him—after the money he's spent this summer he doesn't have a leg to stand on. How was the camp?"

"So-so."

"You look remarkably well."

"Give me time."

"What's that supposed to mean?"

"Nothing."

She decided there was no point in closing the house for a few weeks after she left and then opening it again when school started and Terry and Beth were back, so that was how I got my three peaceful weeks.

One day I got a postcard from Anne. It only said, *"Et ta piscine, est-ce qu'elle est chauffée?"* It wasn't signed, but I knew who it was from. And if I hadn't known, it was postmarked Philadelphia and I would have known that way. I hadn't thought about anyone from up there, and it seemed like a message from another world, some place I'd visited in a dream.

I wasn't going to answer it, but then I did. First I had to figure out what it said. I thought it asked if *my* swimming pool was heated, but I wasn't absolutely sure. So I went to the library at the Four Arts and a lady there told me that was right.

Then I got a postcard of Worth Avenue, and wrote Anne's address on the place they have for that. Lattimore had given it to me and I had kept it. On the message part I wrote only one word, *"Oui."* I looked it up in a dictionary at the Four Arts to make sure I had it spelled right.

I put the card she had sent me up in the drawer where I keep my grandfather's watch. It's a drawer in one of the bureaus in my room and there are only two things in it—the watch and the postcard.

Charles drove me to the post office and I mailed the card I'd written to her. When I came out of the post office it was very hot and I stood in the doorway for a minute trying to decide how to spend the rest of the day. I had quite a few choices, but none of them were exactly what I wanted to do.